FALLING
ANIMALS

FALLING ANIMALS

SHEILA ARMSTRONG

BLOOMSBURY CIRCUS
LONDON · OXFORD · NEW YORK · NEW DELHI · SYDNEY

BLOOMSBURY CIRCUS
Bloomsbury Publishing Plc
50 Bedford Square, London, WC1B 3DP, UK
29 Earlsfort Terrace, Dublin 2, Ireland

BLOOMSBURY, BLOOMSBURY CIRCUS and the Bloomsbury Circus logo
are trademarks of Bloomsbury Publishing Plc

First published in Great Britain 2023

'In the Storm' from 'The Skelligs' by Eiléan Ní Chuilleanáin from *Collected Poems*
(2020) by kind permission of the author and The Gallery Press, Loughcrew, Oldcastle,
County Meath, Ireland

A catalogue record for this book is available from the British Library

ISBN: HB: 978-1-5266-3585-3; TPB: 978-1-5266-3584-6; EBOOK: 978-1-5266-3583-9;
EPDF: 978-1-5266-6607-9

2 4 6 8 10 9 7 5 3

Typeset by Integra Software Services Pvt. Ltd.
Printed and bound in Great Britain by CPI Group (UK) Ltd, Croydon CRO 4YY

To find out more about our authors and books visit www.bloomsbury.com
and sign up for our newsletters

What am I doing here, says the old strong voice,
the wave reaching and snatching
around the pinnacles, faltering and returning
to fling its quilt across the sloping stone
where in the softer days the seal took a rest;
so it wells up, squirting up roses in its fall,
trying again, the awful repeated recoil,
and where is truth under the slamming and roaring,
it wants to know, and *where,*
where is pity now? Gone below,
wiped from the view, and indeed
what has happened to time, as the day's news
is repeated, bellowing like the storm?

> Eiléan Ní Chuilleanáin, 'The Skelligs:
> In the Storm'

'It's no fish ye're buying – it's men's lives.'

> Sir Walter Scott, *The Antiquary*

for my parents

ONE

the collector

First, there is a seal with no eyes.

It is a spring tide, the beach is shrinking to a silvery half-moon, and the sheets of rock above the tideline are turning black with the unfamiliar spray. Out over the deep water, the dawn light is stretched out and thin; only the iron tip of a shipwreck is visible above the waves. Further out, the tent pole of a lighthouse props up the sky, and from there, the horizon curves into a horseshoe, all the way around the world and back to the dark anchor of the eyeless seal.

A white van is making its way down the narrow, green-spined road to the deserted beach. In the soft, unsteady sand, each turn the driver makes must be a slow and careful adjustment, as the shifting forest of dunes is precarious at the best of times. Harsh winters have lashed chunks out of them, and each day the shoreline morphs and changes further. A recent summer storm has left debris above the tideline: the delicate shells of sea urchins and clumps of orange-brown seaweed, as thick as matted hair.

The driver left with the early August dawn to get to the beach before the first walkers appeared. He drives cautiously; a few wheel-spinning moments in the dunes had set his heart pounding. There will be a man with a tractor to pull him out if he gets stuck – there is always a man with a tractor around, collecting oysters from the half-submerged traps – but Frank is booked in for a drop-off at the incinerator before lunch, and a delay would mean more paperwork.

He tries to park as close to the carcass as he can. Through the windscreen, the seal looks so pristine it might have just pulled itself out of the ocean to rest, propped up in an alert position, empty eye sockets staring blankly out to sea. Closer up there will be flies, he knows from experience, squirming things to pull the seeds of life from death. The county council usually ignore these strandings, if they hear about them at all; they are happy to wait for the animal to quietly decompose or leave on the next tide. But this seal, a casualty of the storm, has wedged itself firmly between two small mounds of rock above the shore-line and seems determined to cling on. The village overlooking the beach is teeming with tourists, with delicate stomachs and a tendency to complain, so Frank has been sent to remove what the sea will not wash away.

A gust snatches the van door out of his hands; he lets it close on top of himself, using his hips to catch the heavy force of the swing. He pulls his kit out of the van, a tarpaulin unfurling to whip in the wind like a thick, black spinnaker. Gloves. Face mask. Shovel. Bungee cords. Disinfectant. The hydraulics wheeze as the rear ramp lowers; it catches on one side, but he stamps on it with his boots until it is level with the beach. He weighs the tarp down with some metal straps and goes closer to inspect the carcass. A pair of red-beaked gulls lift their heads and scream at him as he approaches, clattering their way into the air, disappearing behind swathes of marram grass further up the beach.

Up close, the seal's skin is sleek-dark, but swollen, like a burnt sausage; islands of black floating on cracks of red lava. The empty, gull-pecked sockets are deep tunnels shaded with garnet. He reaches out a boot and taps the bulky body – once, twice, and again with the other foot – to get a sense of the weight and heft of it. Thankfully, the days following the unseasonable storm have been scorching hot, so the sun and salt have dried the carcass out. Many years hauling fallen livestock has taught him that cattle and horses are prone to leakage. Sheep with heavy winter wool are the worst, like a kitchen sponge that looks bone dry but spills out foulness once lifted. Frank considers just loosening the seal enough for it to roll back down the beach, to feed the crabs and little lives of the ocean. But the council expects an invoice from the incinerator, so a seal he must produce.

As the shrouded sun appears above the cliffs, he begins to tease the sand around the seal with his shovel. He breathes through his masked mouth as he works, testing and loosening, peeling the carcass away from the sand. As he suspected, the underside has begun to blister and rot. If the sand is fouled deeply enough, he will need to take a layer of it away with him too. Sandhoppers emerge as he disturbs the scene, their small, fingernail bodies unfolding and leaping Olympic heights into the air. Crabs too, greedy little things still grabbing clawfuls of flesh as his spade comes down a hair's breadth from them. He splits one cleanly in two; its brain doesn't immediately realise it is dead, and both claws still extend and return to their half of the alien mouth.

He goes back to the van and gathers up the black tarp. Lays it out alongside the carcass. Levers the hind flippers up with the blunt edge of his shovel, kicks the heavy material further underneath them. The seal rocks and settles on the tarp, and its empty eye sockets catch the rising sun as it batters its way out from under the clouds. The redness of them surprises him – bright crimson rather than brown and old, as if a heart was still beating slowly somewhere.

He heaves one end of the tarp until the seal is face down, rolling the carcass up like a fat cigar. The seal's skin is as crisp as the surface of an iced pond; his gloved palms leave grooves of damage in the blubber. He folds the tarp over the ends and secures it with bungee cords. The wrapped shroud marks a gully in the sand behind it as he drags it over to the van. The weight seems concentrated, as if there is a weight deep in the seal's stomach and the layers of fat and skin around it are all to protect a cold, iron core.

When the carcass is neatly packed away, Frank stops to catch his breath in the strengthening wind. In the distance, there are already a few Sunday-morning walkers trickling down the steep beach path, below a line of caravans that poke up from the cliff like teeth in a black jawbone. The sun has pulled visitors from all over the country; whole families have arrived with their bikes and barbeques and dogs and noise. The village on the cliffs, usually sullen and grey, is basking in the heat like a dozing lizard.

Last week's storm seems distant now, as if it happened in a different country. He had heard the howl of the wind from his bedroom, even far inland, so the ferocity on the north-west coastline, in this exposed place, must have been awesome. He had almost roused his wife to listen to it, but had instead dozed off again, drifting on the steady whum-whum of the gusts. He wonders if it was the waves or the wind that forced his seal out of the water. About half a kilometre inland are the remains of a whale's skeleton, where rocks shaped like bones, or bones shaped like rocks, fall in rough formation. How far would the sea have to rise to drop it there? Even today's spring tide falls well short and still has the wild border of dunes to cover. As he considers the distances, he sips from the flask of tea his wife made for him sometime during the night and feels the dull stirring of his affection for her, like the shifting of continents.

While he worked, the high tide has slipped away to reveal a distant sandbank. Out there, chunks of the shipwreck are beginning to emerge, revealing the remains of iron ribs and a fragmented hull. Black, glossy seals lollop out of the water on to the sand beside it, turning to stare at him curiously. He raises two fingers to the animals: an acknowledgement of their loss, an apology for disturbing their fallen comrade. He picks up his shovel and goes back to attack the stained soil that was underneath the carcass. Traces an extended outline with the sharp edge of the blade, pulling it behind him in a large circle. Digs into the marked-off space, lifts dark, iodine sods and turns them over.

After a quarter of an hour he takes another break. The sand is stonier than it looks, he is older than he feels, and he has raised a sweat. At the far side of fifty, Frank now only does the odd call-out, leaving the rest to the younger boys – the ones who can laugh as they wash the blood and gore off, who can keep a wall in their heads between the slaughter yard and the other parts of their lives. He comes in for the drop-offs and paperwork, and then home again to a kitchen where reds and browns are the untainted colours of garden flowers and his wife's freshly baked bread.

Halfway along the visible sliver of beach is an outcrop of rocks that juts from the cliffs, bending downwards into the water. A figure in a wetsuit is feeling its way up the steps cut out of the rock. The swimmer moves out along the edge, a reversed silhouette against the landscape. Further inland, there is not enough light yet to excavate gullies and cliffs; the mountains are grey-green against the sky with no real depth to them. Frank reaches out his arm and traces them as if he is holding a scalpel, half-expecting the canvas to fall away, revealing the wooden shafts of the backdrop. The swimmer on the rocks bends to slap at the water with the palm of his hand, then wets the back of his neck.

The faint sound of whirring passes overhead as a helicopter swings wide above the lighthouse, around the village squatting on the cliffs, and disappears inland behind a bank of clouds. Frank finds himself glad, so glad, that his passengers don't wear clothes and shoes, don't have pale-shocked husbands or wailing mothers standing by as he pulls them from where they have fallen. Once, he was called out after a thunderstorm, when a stallion had slipped its line and leapt from a cliff, white-eyed and wild with terror. Its owner said it jumped so high it had almost, almost flown.

He turns back to the half-dug circle of ashy sand. Behind him there is a splash as the swimmer enters the water.

Before he leaves, he sprays the sand with disinfectant, and watches carefully as the sandhoppers scatter away from the light mist, a handful writhing and dying on the freshly turned surface. The gulls glare at him from a safe distance away. He sits on the ramp of the van for a moment to finish his steel flask of tea, pulls off his gloves and rubs lavender-scented lotion into his fingers. He turns his head from side to side until the bones at the bottom of his neck crack in a soft, unsatisfying way. The swimmer in the water is breast-stroking out to a distant marker, their capped head like the angry tip of a boil jutting from the waves. He drains his flask and stands to leave.

The tide has slipped away further, and the marks left by his van's wheels are clear and stark above the tideline. Frank tries to return across the beach along the same path, lining the wheels up with the tyre tracks, but it is impossible; the new ruts are deeper than the old with the added weight of the seal. In the front of the van, a pine air freshener bobs on a length of elastic, but the smell has long been used up, breath by breath by breath.

Behind him, all along the exposed beach, black dots of birds search the glint and melt of the stranded clumps of seaweed. The sand uncovered by the tide becomes wind-rippled, like a bared sheet of muscle. At the southerly edge of the beach, silt-rich drainage water seeps from the cliff down a rocky channel and into the ocean. It is barely a trickle in the summer, but in winter it floods and seethes with run-off, cutting out a new shape every time it gushes across the sand like a floodplain. Along the edges, a line of translucent sandhoppers are leaping from the space where a seal's carcass once lay, slow and careful jumps, from one pile of seaweed to the next, searching, moving in a black procession towards the dunes.

At the top of the stream, where the water disappears into vertical cracks in the sheer cliff, there is a sagging of marram grass, a clearing that has been flattened by the unexpected weight of a body. The man in the dunes is sitting serenely, legs crossed at the ankles and fingers interlaced, as if he is simply resting, two half-lidded eyes staring out to sea. The gulls are still circling, cautious after the van's departure, unsure if the intruder with the shovel will return. But they will eventually grow brave again, brave enough to investigate, as the morning light falls strangely on a day-old face.

the witness

The swimmer dives from the rocks into the freezing water and explodes like a depth charge. A few heart-beats later he surfaces, gasping, shaking the water from his face.

From the beach, Oona watches her grandson tread water, panting as he waits for the cold shock to pass. There are leapers and there are creepers, he once told her: those who get it over with in one go, and those that creep into the water, step by step, letting each part of their body adjust. She herself has always believed that change will come, one way or another, but there is no need to leap headfirst into uncertainty.

She counts her steps as she walks along the beach and breathes deeply, letting her chest fill up with the tight chill before the heat of the day arrives in earnest. Her grandson keeps pace with her, erupting out of the water in a butterfly stroke then disappearing again. These Sunday-morning swims have become a ritual for the two of them, ever since her heart began to flicker and gasp last year. The doctor prescribed a palmful of drugs, her grown children prescribed a regime of fruit and yoga; these weekly walks are the compromise, a way of keeping the peace.

Further up the beach, a white van passes parallel to her, weaving around lumps of cast-out seaweed and scribbles of driftwood. She tries to get the driver's attention, points towards the darker, firmer sand that would give the tyres a better grip. But the driver ignores her and continues towards the narrow path up the cliffs, the wheels throwing up fountains of grey powder. Oona shakes her head at this reckless-ness. She often sees cars lodged in the sand, wheels spinning, especially in the summer when tourists try to drive straight down on to the beach and instead get caught in the dunes. She watches them heave and struggle, and if the mood takes her, she calls for one of the oyster farmers to pull them out. If not, she leaves them arguing in her wake.

Up on the cliff, a handful of caravan roofs are glinting in the sun, and the car park will soon fill up. The village beyond is still shaded – cold, draughty buildings that spiral away from the seafront like the whorl of a shell; at its centre, a café, a pub and a small supermarket arranged around an empty green. Most of the other shops remain shuttered, even years after the worst of the recession. The docks that used to swarm with fishing boats are empty now, and the thick fug of salt and blood has long faded. A newly opened motorway sweeps north and south to the main destinations, cutting the village off like a dried-up oxbow lake.

But it is summer now and in summer the tourists still manage to wriggle in, as inevitable as rats to a barn. The caravan park fills up, tents sprout like cabbages, and the half-empty housing estate on the hill bursts into life. In warm weather, the beach is black with people, and even on cold days there are swimmers in thick robes and too-loud voices, their hair shaggy with salt. The handful of guesthouses are bursting at the seams and the buses that stop on the cliff seem to disgorge more and more people each day.

Oona finds it disconcerting: she might walk from one end of the village to the other without seeing a single person she knows. She has lived in the village for seventy-odd years and knows it by heart: every scrap of the ground, every rumour and fireside story, every branching of bloodlines, witnessed every triumph and every loss. The politicians talk about tourism as the life force of the community, but as she sees it, they manage perfectly well for nine months of the year without strangers tramping and littering and shrieking and letting their dogs shit everywhere.

But she has the beach to herself, for now, another reason she insists on coming so early; they will be home by the time the children arrive to dig furrows and trace their initials in the sand. She lengthens her stride to step over the wet splatter of a lion's-mane jellyfish, red veins fanned out like the spokes of an umbrella. There was a time when a jellyfish cast up on the shore was an interesting thing, worth a poke with a stick, but the last few years the water has been seething with them, the beach glowing electric-blue with man o' wars. They ride on the warm-blooded storms that nip and change the coastline, and the newspapers proclaim doom and gloom. But there were worse storms when Oona was growing up, storms that washed whole buildings into the sea. Her own mother had the roof blown off the farmhouse when she was a child, and there were worse heatwaves then too, summers so hot her skin blistered off her back. But nobody wants to hear it: her children and grandchildren roll their eyes at her and predict the end of the world.

She raises her hand to salute as the coastguard's helicopter passes in another slow loop, then heads back towards the distant inland airport. A training exercise: it is too early in the day for there to be a kayaker caught by the tide or a child stranded on an inflatable raft. She glances out to sea to check on her grandson, finds his yellow hat and black goggles amongst the white horses. In the water, he surfaces to reorient himself against the distant mountains, then dives under again.

She is almost parallel with the lumps of iron appearing from the retreating tide when she sees it. A pair of gulls start up from the dunes at her approach, screeching in annoyance, and she angles her path towards the dark shape they were investigating. Junk is often thrown up on the beach, barrels and fridges and furniture that have been dumped illegally somewhere up the coast. Closer up, she is surprised to see the shape resolve into a mannequin. It is sitting propped up against a sand dune with its hands folded and bare feet crossed, perfectly serene, and she wonders at the neatness, that the sea spat it out so delicately.

The truth of what she is seeing comes over her slowly, although she holds on for a moment longer, runs through the few remaining shopfronts in the village, trying to think if any might be missing a mannequin. Then she lets the fiction trickle away and accepts that what she is looking at is a corpse. The body is that of a man around her own age, grey-haired and hollow-cheeked. His skin is ghostly white, slick as ceramic, and his clothes hang loosely, as if they are a size too big. His eyes are squinting out to sea at something just out of sight, and there is the faint hint of a smile on his face. Beside him are a pair of boots, the socks neatly stuffed inside, and a jacket, folded just as neatly. Numbly, she pats the pockets down for a wallet, a phone, something to identify the man, as if the jacket were left behind in the pub. A thick gold ring plunks into the sand at her feet, and some manic instinct makes her try to replace it on the man's hand. But the rigor of death has frozen his hands in place, and his ring finger – the whole finger, from the very base of the knuckle – is missing, the skin long-healed, smooth and taut over the nub of bone.

She stares at the ring in the palm of her hand and realises there will be an empty bed somewhere this morning, a ticking time bomb of grief. She has joined many a search crew combing the shoreline for a missing person, has heard the mournful shout go up, seen loved ones collapse as the news was broken. She takes off her cardigan and presses it to her chest, as if the cloth will protect her from that faraway, abstract discovery, bows her head in a silent prayer.

Her grandson staggers out of the beating waves; he saw her stop and bend over, clasping at her heart, and imagined the worst. He comes alongside and touches her shoulder in relief, then lets out a hard pulse of breath through his nose, bends to shake the man, as if to rouse him from a deep sleep, heaves the upper torso up off the ground and lets it drop against the sand again. His trembling fingers reach for a pulse.

Oona could have told him not to bother. In the man's face, she sees a phantom – not her late husband, lying so serenely in their bed one morning, but one sixty years older: her cousin, hauled up on the pier after disappearing under a moored boat; her aunt's shrieks splitting the air; the limpness of the girl's soft body that had so recently been contorting in the sun; the men pumping at her and the creak of her ribs. And in the dead man's cheeks, the same blue tinge, but all around them silent, except for the gulls.

———————

On the way home, her grandson shivering in the seat beside her, they are quiet. He had pronounced himself too shaken to change out of his wetsuit, and a wet stain is creeping across the seat. The salt will stain the fabric, Oona knows, but she doesn't mention it, even though her new jeep is her pride and joy, another mark against her in her children's eyes. Instead, she rests a hand on his shoulder as they drive.

There is an aching sadness, in the car, but it is untethered: the dead man is a stranger to them. But still, they feel a tenderness towards him, as if he were a bird caught in their kitchen curtains. She rolls down the windows to let the breeze in, to let the grief fly out. It will make a good story to tell in the pub, she thinks, then scolds herself for even considering that, for her callousness, her disrespect. But all she can think of is a drink, a stiff whiskey to soften the stark image of the corpse that appears every time she closes her eyes.

The bar is wedged, even though it has just gone lunchtime. The crowd is made up mostly of tourists, spillover from the caravan park and the holiday homes. The adults roar at each other and clank pints; children loop around their ankles and tear at packets of crisps as if they were made of gold. Oona finds one or two locals in the front room and shoves her way towards them; they clear a stool for her at the bar. The barman, a dark, olive-skinned man, pulls a glass of stout for her and leaves it to settle.

Word has spread of an accident on the beach that morning, but there are few details, and her account is taken and tasted and discussed in full. She tells them about the man's posture, his neat pile of clothes, his poor blue face. She even tells them about her own madness with the ring – like poor Jackie Kennedy trying to put her husband's brain back in, a man offers. The barman reaches for a dusty bottle on the top shelf, pours her a whiskey for the shock, which she drinks in one go.

The dead man is not a local, they all decide; Oona of all people would have recognised him if he was. She dips her head demurely, accepting this praise as her due. But not a tourist either, she offers, or someone would have reported him missing by now. They shrug and stare into their glasses. When the hourly news comes on the radio, the children are hushed, but there is nothing on the bulletin. We'll know more by morning, they nod to each other.

Word has spread in the village and the six o'clock church bells are silent out of respect – not that they're proper bells any more, Oona says, it's all done by a machine these days, the new parish priest has told her. What has the world come to when even bells can't be trusted, she asks the crowd, and strangers show up dead on the beach? Each time somebody new enters the front room of the bar, she begins the story again, and she is still repeating herself when the barman quietly phones for her son to come pick her up.

———————

Down at sea level the air had been perfectly still, so still that she could hear the whine of a car being driven too fast on the road that leads into the village. She counted the seconds between the first noise and the appearance of the blue lights along the cliff path, like the time between a bolt of lightning and its rumble. But the speeding police car didn't use its siren: whatever had happened had already happened.

Before she rang the Gardaí, she replaced the ring in the dead man's pocket, then stepped away to gather herself. Her grandson said she shouldn't have disturbed the scene of the crime, as if it were something from a television show, rather than the cold, hard reality in front of them. As the sun rose higher, the corpse seemed almost ridiculous against the washed-out backdrop of mountains and sand dunes; an anomaly, a heavy weight in a stretched sheet.

When the lights appeared in the car park, her grandson walked up the steep path to meet the Gardaí, his wetsuit flapping around his waist like an injured octopus. And while she waited alone, the sun dipped and surfaced from behind the clouds, and she had to touch the sitting figure's face just one more time, because in the full light of day the man could have just been resting there, back pressed against the sand dune, gazing out to sea.

But he was as white and as cold as bone. As white and as cold as bone.

the doctor

The red-brown earth of the cliff face is pocked
with ancient rabbit holes that have been softened by
rains into gentle indentations. As the slope rises, the
soil splits and furrows, growing ever steeper, until it
reaches an overhang capped with sun-yellow grass.

Teresa stares up at the cliff for a full half hour,
mapping the trajectory a human body would take if it
were to fall. There is no barrier between the edge and
the sudden drop; a racing child could easily slip over,
or an adult lose their balance and spin backwards, arms
windmilling. They might bounce off an outcropping
here, rotate around the jut of an ancient iron mooring
post, fall spreadeagled amongst the marram grass.

But for the corpse to land so neatly, sitting slouched against a sand dune with its hands clasped, jacket folded beside it? It is unlikely, but not impossible.

If not an accident, then an altercation is her next guess. There are no visible bruises, patches of skin sloughed away or red slashes of blood in the sand. But that does not mean there was no violence. The dead man is perhaps in his late sixties, thin and frail even before death and gravity pulled his flesh away from his bones. There would not have been much fight in him. Teresa tells the forensic technicians to finger-print the sleeves and the wrists; in her mind's eye she sees the murderer neatening the corpse, arranging the hands out of guilt. But there are no fresh footprints around the scene, except those of the two witnesses currently having their statements taken. They will have their shoes measured and compared to the prints in the sand, to see if any are unaccounted for, but this line of thinking doesn't feel right to her. The man himself left no prints; logically, she knows the waves and wind likely erased them from the soft sand, but still, it adds to the strangeness of the scene.

Drowning was her first instinct, and as a pathologist, Teresa mistrusts her first instincts as a matter of course. It would have to be a recent submersion for the body to be cast out so pristinely by the tide. A body will float at first, and there is a chance to find it easily, a chance for a speedy resolution. But then it will sink again, be lost for a time, then slowly rise as the chemicals and gases push out and up. She's seen a hundred drownings, if not more, but only since she came west, to this wild, remote place. Before, in the cities, there were murders and violence, an epidemic of overdoses. But here, she has become an expert in the slow mundanity of drownings.

The Gardaí have marked off the scene with their yellow plastic tape and blocked the corpse from view with their vans, heading off the families that were gathering with their towels and bodyboards for another scorching day. Still, a small, determined crowd is watching her from the clifftop. At least from the base of the cliff, their chatter is flattened to a low buzz – her job should be done in quiet, ticking through possibilities, ruling things out.

Sergeant Gavin Young watches her too, although he tries to hide it by pacing the perimeter and arguing with onlookers. He is thick as a tree trunk, pale, fair-haired and sweating in the growing heat, although he has damp armpits even on the mildest day. This morning – her day off – he rang her twice in the space of an hour, once to inform her that she was required at the scene of a possible crime, the second time to ask if she planned on joining them at any stage this year. Her teenage daughter had watched her leave with hooded eyes, hungover from whatever bar had let her in the night before; Teresa's own head throbbed from a fireside bottle of merlot. There will be another argument between them this evening, as inevitable as the rising sun, and like the sunlight, it will touch on everything but move nothing.

Gavin notices her eyes on him and dips back under the barrier tape to approach, asks what she thinks they are dealing with. He looks at her expectantly, hoping for a quick answer, something that can be neatly filed away. She just shakes her head. The puzzle has sparked a small throb of pleasure in her stomach, a revving of her brain. Her eyes flicker around the scene, gathering up little pieces of the sky, sea, sand: details that will tell her a story, a story about the dead man sitting so serenely on the beach.

———

The body lies supine on the hospital slab, and every time her phone rings she expects it to be Gavin with a name, a family, a history. Or even just a request for an update: he tends to call her while she is working, to check in, as if he is her supervisor and she is an intern on her first day. She dislikes the man, but he knows everyone in the wider area, knows what strings to pull and where to apply pressure. *You're the scientist and I'm the people person*, he once told her. All my best friends are dead, as the pathologist said to the policeman.

She is surprised that nobody has claimed the body so far. Gavin didn't recognise him as a local, but the village is overflowing with people, tourists both national and international, and he is busy checking the guesthouses and caravan park. Teresa has this man pegged as a foreigner, not that that is a particularly scientific estimation, but she feels the rightness of it. *Unknown body*, then, she puts on the top of her file, but leaves a blank space to fill in details later.

His clothes give no clues – a white shirt and dark trousers, brand new and well made, but dry, with no salt stains to suggest that they spent time in the water. Strangely, the labels have been removed, snipped away from the fabric precisely, to the very last thread. There is no wallet, no phone, not even the usual detritus of pocket lining – ticket stubs, coins, loose fluff. Just a thick gold ring in the breast pocket of his jacket, but, curiously, the man is missing the ring finger on his left hand. A call comes from forensics to say that the man's fingerprints are not in any database, and those on the ring match one of the witnesses, who confesses to touching it when questioned. This interference annoys her; she handles each item of evidence carefully before slipping it into a plastic sleeve for storage.

The autopsy only offers her more unknowns. There are no signs of classical saltwater drowning, which put her first instinct to bed, as she knew it would. And no blunt-force injuries to suggest a fall from a high place. Nothing, either, to signal an assault with fists or a weapon. There are old injuries, yes, bones that broke and healed again, scars and burns and thickened skin. His body is sparsely dotted with tattoos that probably meant something to someone, but they have faded with age and are distorted by illness. The man had recently lost weight, his clothes hang loosely on him, and there is wastage in his arms and legs. Signs of a hard life, but a lot of lives are hard.

The toxicology report is negative for drugs – not a single painkiller, sedative or stimulant, not even paracetamol for the pain. Because she finds a lot of pain. Carcinomas, so many that she underlines the word *multiple* twice in her report. He must have been delirious with it; a brave man, or madman, or something else altogether to be upright and walking around with tumours clinging to him like barnacles.

Her own father demanded fistfuls of morphine, but still died screaming in his own bed from the rot in his bones; her mother slipped away quietly and calmly in a hospital room. When she first met her husband, he asked her how she wanted to die, as if this was a question that he put to every woman he met. Teresa was just a medical student then, but his question triggered something in her, just because she couldn't answer it. Even as a child, answering questions was her favourite game, something she begged from any visitor to their home. *Ask me something, ask me*, as if she was a bottomless pit that needed to be filled with knowledge that she could then regurgitate for approval. Her husband's lack of interest in this endless accumulation of facts was a relief, a contrast to the incessant ticking of her own brain. Twenty years later, his love for her is still simple; hers is a constantly changing thing.

After the autopsy, she closes the body up, lines the thorax with sutures in the shape of a tuxedo. She covers it, rolls it into an aluminium drawer for storage; if it isn't claimed soon, she will have to contact an embalmer herself, and each day will take it further and further from recognition.

On her paperwork, she comes to the blank box where she is to fill in the cause of death, pauses to collect her thoughts. Not suicide, nor homicide, nor accident, as far as she can see. Just a body full of pain, breaking down into pieces, but no sign that death was directly caused by the cancer itself. The pose of the corpse – neatly seated, almost polite, as if it didn't want to make a fuss – unnerves her, as if the man had just sat down and decided to die. But she cannot write that down; the jury is waiting.

The sergeant's eyebrows come together into one hard line when she presents him with the autopsy results, and he asks if she is sure. She isn't, of course, isn't sure at all, but his questioning makes her bristle and dig in her heels. He does not like untidy results, or difficult questions, or mysteries that can't be solved by battering a confession out of somebody. But still, she cannot make up facts that are not there.

Death by natural causes.

A month later the body goes unidentified and unmarked into a public grave outside the village, preserved for disinterment, should it become necessary. When she asks the sergeant for updates on the investigation, she can feel the frustration radiating off him in waves. The public appeals have thrown up some leads – dementia patients that have wandered off, missing persons who were last seen parked near a shoreline – but none of them match up with the strange facts of the case. And, as time ticks on, they are running out of ideas.

It is September now, and her daughter Nessa has begun her final year of secondary school. She is bright, too bright for her own good, according to her teachers, but she is raw and easily bruised, like a half-peeled mango. At seventeen, Nessa is too young and too old, too naïve and too cynical, and Teresa cannot find the words to make her daughter understand how cruel the world can be to bright women.

The small catchment area of the north-west seemed appealing, compared to the huge workloads in the city. More free time to spend with her steadfast husband and difficult daughter; an office door that could close firmly at the end of the day. A chance to step back after the hectic first decades of her career, maybe even make some friends. Her husband thinks she spends too much time alone, drinks too much, works too hard. Part of the agreement they made when they moved here was that she would try to find a life outside of her work, go to dinner dates and garden parties and book clubs. And she has tried, even though her disinterest in the workings of other people's lives was part of the reason she chose this branch of medicine in the first place. She even joined a sea swimming club, but the involuntary gasp her body let out when it hit the cold water felt too much like losing control.

The coroner's inquest will be in January, and she will have to face a court and present her findings, cycle through possibilities and probabilities. This is straightforward when a skull has been split open, or a bone is wedged through an organ, or toxicology results are listed in bright red. It is easy, then, to sit in front of a jury with a flipboard, trace fractures and chemical spikes and map haematomas, with black-inked facts to shore her up. But this is not straightforward, and Teresa finds herself poring over her files again and again, searching for something she has missed. She hates uncertainty, hates to leave a life flapping around without a pinned-down ending, without that most final of answers.

Again and again, she comes back to the man's posture, the unnatural serenity of it. As if he was exactly where he wanted to be.

the son

The noticeboard is just outside the door of the supermarket where he works, above a green postbox built into a low wall. Usually, the board is filled with tearaway slips for piano lessons and French grinds and lost cats. It isn't until Mitchell is clearing off some of the older, sun-yellow signs that he gets a good look at the poster half-hidden behind a restaurant flyer.

HAVE YOU SEEN THIS PERSON? it says, above a gritty, black and white still from a CCTV camera – a shot of a tall, thin man with grey hair walking across a courtyard, shoulders hunched and head down, with the blunt nose of a bus in the foreground.

When Mitchell's mother gets brain scans, she describes how the contrast dye the doctors use sends a warm wave gushing through her entire body, making it feel like she's wet herself. And when Mitchell looks closely at the blurry figure in profile, he has to look down at his own trousers.

A few days later, he works up the courage to ring the number on the bottom of the poster. Later that afternoon, a burly, fair-haired guard calls into the supermarket and asks him to come down to make a statement. His manager chats to the guard affably about the price of fuel for a few minutes, but when they leave, he narrows his eyes and leans out the front door to watch them walk away.

As they get into the marked car, teenage girls on their lunchbreak call low, sarcastic ooohs from their perches, like a flock of eider ducks. It is late October, the air is wet ice, but still the girls have bare legs above their high navy socks. They eat greasy chips from the café on the square and suck the salt from their fingers. Mitchell is only a few years older than them, but to him they seem like dressed-up dolls in their tartan kilts and heavy school jumpers. But at least they are familiar; the sheer mass of them, their easy ebb and flow. His own friends, back in West Virginia, have spread out like the prongs of a rake, into universities or the army or marriages or opioid habits. And he is here, alone, at the edge of the world.

At the station, the guard disappears and a woman takes his name and details. She tells him that he better do an interview so they can get it all sorted out. In the chill of the waiting area, his heels play a samba against the tiles. A large, old-fashioned clock ticks loudly, off beat. People come in and out, picking up blank sheets of paper. He begins to cry, softly, and the guards at the counter look at each other, startled. One leaves to murmur a few words to a silhouette behind a frosted window. The tempo in the station picks up a notch.

Behind the interview-room door, it is freezing.

So you say you saw this man?

Sorry, is all Mitchell can say to the guard, mashing at his eye sockets with the base of his palms. The man is less cordial away from the casual banter at the supermarket; his words are sharper and faster, and his stoutness seems more like bulk.

What are you sorry for, lad? Best to get it out.

Mitchell tries to pull the wet flood back up his nose; almost chokes on the thickness of it. He begins to hiccup, the hard, painful sort that feels like swallowing a stone.

Did he say something to you? Make you angry? We can't help you unless you tell us.

He is so, so sorry.

———

On the day his mother got her wheelchair, Mitchell watched her roll it into the house, testing the push and drag of it. Her fingers slotted into the grips on the handles, and, just for a moment, she looked absolutely terrified. Then she noticed him looking, swung the chair around to jam it up against his shins and told him to get in. He backed away, but she followed him like she was shoving a shopping cart towards the checkout. He sighed, recognising the playful crease in her eyes, and carefully lowered himself into the fabric seat.

His mother spun the chair around, clumsy with his added weight, and looked at him critically, up and down. He raised his arms above his head to stretch, settling in as if it were a throne. She snorted and turned the chair again, slower this time, and began to wheel him through the kitchen. His vantage point was only a little lower than usual, but the kitchen was transformed, like he was seeing up someone's nose. The blue and white pattern on the tiles above the cabinets now looked like feathers instead of leaves. The undersides of the cabinets were dirty, and he made a mental note to wipe them before his mother noticed. On the fridge, the I'M NOT DRUNK – I JUST HAVE MS magnet his mother had ordered online somehow looked less funny; the font seemed sharper, more pointed.

His mother turned the chair until it faced the three wide, shallow steps up into the hallway. The house, like all the others in the estate, is shaped like the path of a knight in a chess game – a small, protruding kitchen perpendicular to a long hallway where the bedrooms and painting studio are located, connected by the steps. He recently sat on those steps for over an hour while she perched on the table with a cooling mug of tea, arguing about him dropping out of college. The night before, she had been trapped in the bathtub for three hours, the water chill and scummy, until he came home from work and lifted her out. She cried then, wild and hard, and he held her, dried her hair, pushed her feet gently into her pyjamas one leg at a time.

The next day, she insisted that she didn't need a carer; that he should go back to the States instead of wasting his life, wasting his brains, wasting his youth. He said it was his own life to waste, raising his voice, even while she stayed calm, on the outside at least. When she does lash out, it comes like a scalding cloud of steam, a long-banked eruption, but that day she was firm and sure of her words. He still won the argument, though, because what can you do when you leave your son behind on a different continent, and your authority with it? Finding that out had led to a few difficult years, but they had come out stronger on the other side, allies against the rest of the fucking world. Including, but not limited to, the biggest bastard of all, multiple sclerosis.

When his mother's consultant had gently suggested that the progression of the disease indicated she might soon need to consider occasionally using a wheelchair, his very first thought had been those three fucking steps. And so, he had begged some wood from his manager and tried, with frantic energy, to build a ramp – just a plank of plywood, really, but he had secured it underneath with posts and wood glue. He hadn't said a word to his mother all the while, fussing with his borrowed tools; anything to avoid seeing the fear in her eyes.

The slope was shallow, but from this angle, sitting in the wheelchair, it looked much steeper. His mother pulled the chair back for momentum, then put all her weight behind it and started rolling towards the ramp. They both began making a low rumble of preparation, and as they hit the first ridge, their voices were rising, wordless, entwined. Mitchell didn't have time to feel afraid: the ramp wobbled under the four wheels, but it held – it held. The chair flew up the slope under her hands and they were roaring, cheering, as she swung it around the corner and let it go. He clattered down the corridor, fast, too fast; he found the side brake and heaved on it, pulling the wheelchair around in a hand-brake turn until he was facing her again, laughing.

She was leaning against the wall, breathing heavily, but already the triumph in her face was fading away. She was staring straight through him, and he could see the glisten of tears in the sleek, wet curve of her eyeball. He got to his feet and came towards her, standing awkwardly about an arm's-length away. A hug could provoke that cloud of steam if he tried it at the wrong time, and every day felt like the wrong time, every word the wrong word.

She gathered herself up with a hard and heavy sigh, walked past him down the hallway, the open backs of her slippers flopping against the wooden floor. She didn't meet her son's eyes as she sat in the chair, pulled off the brake and awkwardly wheeled herself towards her studio. She could reach the handle without having to stand up.

After the door closed behind her, and after some hours alone in the kitchen, Mitchell had pulled out an old notebook and begun to write. He had always loved writing stories, as a child, but in high school he'd become sick of what he was putting on the page, sick of himself. He felt like he was trying to draw water from a deep well with a teaspoon, and the frustration ended in torn pages and notebooks filled with huge black crosses.

When he finished high school, he decided on a whim to apply for a degree in computer science in Ireland. Numbers and straight lines felt easier to control than his own brain, and he told himself the move would be the beginning of a wide, bright future. His mother had recently been diagnosed with MS, which was part of it too; it had set off a mild panic in him, the realisation that he didn't know this woman at all. Any residual resentment he felt towards her softened when he arrived last year and could see how much this wild place suited her, how unhappy she had been with his father.

But on his first day in college, he had felt like a stranded fish, gasping and flailing to get back into the water. He lasted a month before dropping out. Now he can only think about the future in small, manageable mouthfuls; anything more and paralysis settles over him like a greasy membrane.

When he finished writing, he had a silly limerick about her speeding down the motorway in the wheelchair, being pulled over and talking her way out of a ticket. It ended with her flying past the cop so fast he spilled his coffee in his own lap. It was an awkward, childish thing, and covered with scratched-out words, but he wrote it out again on a fresh sheet of paper and slid it under her door. She didn't come out again that evening, but in the morning the poem was pinned to the fridge, behind the I'M NOT DRUNK magnet.

Like I'm five years old again, he commented over breakfast.

Maybe you haven't done anything worth saving since then.

She was smiling as she said it, and she reached out and grabbed his hand tightly, just for a second. And then she was off to the hardware store because she had more energy in the mornings and she needed more paint thinner. He had smiled along with her, but as the door closed behind her, his face began a gentle droop downwards, like an unpinned sheet of fabric.

He walked to work along the cliff path and looked out at the grey, grey sky. He listened to his manager complain about the weather. He wiped down the deli counter. He scanned in fourteen cans of a particular brand of cat food for an elderly woman. When she said they were the only thing her cats would eat, he went into the back and found six more. When he got home, he feigned interest in his mother's day as he made a lentil stew for dinner.

But afterwards, in the garden, he slammed the lid of the compost bin down so hard on the onion peelings that a couple of crows startled from the trees. He slammed it again, and again, and again, until the handle broke off in his hand.

***

He had cycled out to the beach that warm summer's evening to clear his head, Mitchell tells the officer, after they get him a drink of water and he wipes his face clean in the station's bathroom.

When he got to the beach, he tossed his bike against a crowded rack, sat in a small hollow in the cliffs with his back pressed against a hummock of grass. There had been caravans, and dogs, and children, and ice-cream vans, and fleets of bicycles, and couples, and elderly walkers, a cacophony of people that flowed around him like disinterested ghosts. He put on a set of headphones and tried to listen to a podcast, but when the speaker's voice trailed away, he couldn't find the energy to change the track and had sat there for an hour with the dead white plastic stuffed into his ears.

He sat and watched the sun go down over the beach, the stranded iron ribs of a derelict ship casting longer and longer shadows. The light began to fade, into a garish, ridiculous sunset; one of those pink-purple explosions that only exist for people like his mother to mimic on canvas. He sat longer, until the crowds drained away, and the sharp black line that signalled the edge of the cliff scrawled itself across his vision, sharper and sharper. It flashed from one end of the world to the other, again and again, like an ink-scribbled pulse, splitting the land from the sky.

The crowds had thinned further, the beach emptied, and his vision darkened into greyscale when a man came into view from under the lip of the cliff, limping over and back, picking through the rocks as the incoming tide pushed him higher up the shoreline. Full darkness had almost fallen, but his white shirt seemed to glow against the grey sand, a jacket folded over his arm. The stranger looked up, as if he felt Mitchell's eyes on him, and although he was too far away to make out the man's expression, it felt like an acknowledgement, an understanding.

He flounders while describing the man to the guards, trying to explain why he had been so stricken by his appearance. His mother gives painting classes in the community centre, and at the end, to give a scene perspective, they add tiny, vague people shaped like carrots – a long, tapering brushstroke for the body, with a dot for the head. But this man hadn't seemed like that.

There was something about him, as if the landscape was there to frame him instead of the other way around.

When the guards ask why he hadn't come forward sooner, he tells them the truth: he heard the news about the body on the beach, but most days he feels like a bystander in his own life, so the possibility of his involvement hadn't registered. He regrets it as soon as the stupid words leave his mouth, so when they ask why he had been upset earlier on, he shrugs and says he doesn't know, that he is stressed, that he hadn't slept well the night before. He doesn't tell them that sometimes the sadness in him feels so heavy, like hot tar, and he tries to vomit it out, hacking over the toilet like a rabid dog. That sometimes, when he is filling hot-water bottles for his mother's lap, he wants to jerk the stream of boiling water out of alignment with the hole and let it run over his fingers, searing his skin all the way down to the clean, white bone.

He doesn't tell them that he had cycled to the beach that day with no particular plan in mind, only that throwing himself off the cliff was an option. It wasn't something he was excited for, something he had gone specially to do, but it was there, available for consideration should he feel that it was the right time. The ribbon of thought had sat in his back pocket all the way down the road, rattling up and over his head with every speed bump, weaving in and out of the spokes of the wheels like a disinterested eel.

But something had shifted as he met the eyes of the man on the beach – that first, finger-bruising hint of movement from a tightly wound screw – and when he finally disappeared from view, Mitchell stood up again to go home. The warmth of the sand had leeched into him, so there was a dark patch where he had been sitting, chilled and shadowed compared to the rest.

And now the man is dead.

The guards make him sign a statement; say they'll be in touch. They are suspicious, he knows that, and he would be suspicious of himself too, crying over a stranger for no good reason. He knows this guilt is irrational, that self-destruction is not contagious, but his brain cannot connect these facts with the churning in his gut. He thinks of all the documentaries he has watched about coerced confessions and planted evidence and false convictions. He wonders if he will end up the subject of one of them in ten years, with a sad and swelling soundtrack, if his mother will live to see him walk out of jail. He has to stop to vomit in the bushes behind the bus stop.

Mitchell doesn't tell his mother about the Garda station, about the statement, about any of it. He tells her he has a cold; his still-swollen sinuses hoarsen his voice convincingly. His dad has sent over some flu drugs from America, as bright and sugary as Skittles, and he takes a handful, hoping to sleep it off. But his brain seems to sweat and hiss like a steam engine in the quiet of the dark. He tries to lull it with the soft blue light of his phone's screen as he scrolls through the dull noise of the internet, reading everything he can find, retaining none of it. Exhausted adrenaline eventually pulls him under and the phone slips out of his grip.

A thump startles him awake in a dreamy terror, sure the stranger on the beach is advancing, crowned in seaweed, seawater dripping from bruised-grey skin, up the ramp towards his bedroom. Then the clunk comes again and it is the closing of the bathroom door and the whisk-whisk of the wheelchair along the darkened corridor.

the driver

There are only a few people giving evidence in the coroner's court: the pathologist, a guard and some witnesses, all shivering in a room with a tall ceiling and a hardwood floor. A lone sprig of leftover tinsel dangles sadly from a window, twisting in the dull January light. An elderly woman takes almost an hour to recount how she found the body, a story that could have been told in ten minutes. When she begins to describe the scene again, the coroner dismisses her, and calls up a skinny young man who seems terrified. His voice is clear, though, as he describes briefly how he saw the man walking along the beach the night before his body was found.

Darragh is the last to testify; he supposes they are moving in reverse chronological order, and he is the last known link in the chain. His evidence is not really evidence at all, rather the lack of it: he is a bus driver, he drove a man from a place to another place, and nothing of interest happened. But the summons had come in the post, and his wife insisted he attend out of civic duty, in the hope he could offer a detail that might help identify the still-anonymous man. Mainly, though, he wants to draw a line under the memory; force it out of his head and into other people's hands, let them do what they will with it.

But sitting there, on the stand, facing the small crowd – a few journalists and members of the public that have wandered in – he wants to start with the comet.

When he was ten years old, the comet had come screaming out of the sky and into a field by his house. The green fireball flew in a low slant across the night, and the boom that followed it had rattled all the teeth in his mouth. But in the memory, almost forty years past, Darragh is not perched in the comfortable darkness behind his own eyes. Rather, he is watching from somewhere over his own shoulders, as if he were a character in a film.

He can see the back of his sleep-mussed head leaning far out of his bedroom window. His father's
arm forcing the kitchen shutters open below him.
He can hear his father cursing in his Donegal Irish,
fragments forced together into an awkward whole;
the short, harsh chain of words ballooning out up
into the sky, trailing the comet until it disappeared
over a distant field.

In the frosty morning, he met up with his friends
Simon and wee Andy, and they went hunting for the
meteorite, divining its path by comparing the angles
of what they had seen from each of their windows.
Andy stuck three nails into the earth to stand for their
houses, tied a piece of string to each nail to mark
the comet's tail and used the point where the three
converged to map the trajectory. Andy went on to be
an architect, which had surprised no one. Simo had
thrown himself into the river a decade later, which
had surprised some of them, Darragh included.

The boys searched all day until, in a hollow outside
a dried-out quarry, they found a huge, reddened
rock that Andy announced was the remains of the
meteor. It had been as tall as their knees, smoothly
cratered, with silvery flecks threaded through
the rust-coloured stone. Simo said the holes were
probably made by space slugs digging tunnels, like
the one that had almost caught the Millennium
Falcon in *The Empire Strikes Back*. Andy told him
that was stupid, and they fell into a shoving match.

While they fought, Darragh put his hand up to the rock, and he could feel the dry flames of space deep in the heart of it. It had sparkled crimson in the weak winter sun, and was the most beautiful thing he had ever, ever seen.

It had taken the three of them an hour to drag the precious thing out of the field, and another hour to tie a net of rope around it and tow it back to Darragh's garage behind their bikes, the boys bouncing and cursing off each other all the way down the country lanes. They had been hot with exertion and pride by the time they managed to roll it into the garage at sunset.

They'd be famous the whole world over, Andy claimed, and rich too. If, Simo argued, a cloud of green spores carrying a toxic alien plague didn't explode out of the rock in the night and spread across all of Ireland. They would have to open the meteorite up, the boys agreed, to see what was inside. They parted ways for dinner; Simo planned to come by with a chisel in the morning and Andy would try to borrow his da's sledgehammer.

But at breakfast the next day, Darragh had seen the front page of the newspaper. A man in a flat cap was pictured holding something heavy in both arms, cradling it like a baby, a wild, proud smile on his face. The rock was ugly and dark with sharp corners where the one in Darragh's garage was red-stained, even and beautiful. The horrible grinning man was

47

standing beside a brown track of exposed dirt in a green field, a tapering skidmark ending in a crater the size of a cow. In the background, someone had tied a tricolour to an upright pitchfork, claiming the site for Ireland. COMET LANDS IN FARMER'S FIELD, said the headline.

Simo and Andy didn't come by with the chisel and sledgehammer, and when Darragh next met them, they didn't bring up the 'comet' waiting for them in his garage. When they had been taken on a school trip to see the *real* comet's landing site the next month, they drifted away from each other in embarrassment while queuing for the bus, only converging again at the chipper on the way home.

And the beautiful, crimson-sparkling rock that was just a rock after all sat in Darragh's parents' garage for twenty years until his mother ordered it rolled out and into the road to make space to store her car.

———

At night, when he can't sleep, Darragh skims through other memories, watching himself as a boy, a teen, a grown man, a father. He replays these moments again and again, trying to note the simple details that twist and braid themselves into a whole. An upside-down rally car in flames off a back road. His own collarbone protruding from his skin like hard, white plastic against the green of a football pitch. A dark flock of birds flying into the engine just a few minutes after take-off on his first transatlantic flight.

But he sees these memories from above, rather than from behind his own eyes, because at some stage in his life he has described them to someone else, and the telling has shaken him loose from that perch. Now, he is just another character in the memory, replaying an endless loop.

This particular story has been told so many times that it has a life of its own, and he will never regain the foothold behind his own eyes. Told first to his supervisor, then to the sergeant, then written down and trapped in words in a statement, sealed with his very own signature. Told to his wife, his siblings, and to his children when they heard the gossip from friends. And still, sometimes at night when he closes his eyes, it begins again.

His first bus route in the morning leaves at five minutes past seven. It's a nice time to drive north. In summer it is bright and by the time he gets to his final stop a third of the day has already passed. In the sleepy dark of winter he can close his eyes to slits and follow the road on autopilot, using a trick his father taught him – put your hands at ten and two, stick up your thumbs, and line them up with the road markings. There are usually only a handful of travellers, and at six in the morning, the journey from Westport to Belfast is blessedly silent, as if it were still part of the private, closed-off time before the day officially starts.

The return route is at five minutes past two in the afternoon, after a hurried lunch in the station's staffroom. At this stage, there is overflow from the ferries that come in from England, and his passengers are usually foreigners. They struggle a little with buying their tickets, wrangling suitcases up the steps of the coach. He tries to flatten his Donegal accent; to speak slowly and smoothly and find patience when they thrust the wrong currency at him.

In this particular memory, it is a bright August afternoon in Belfast. He is sitting in the driver's seat outside the bus station, waiting for the dashboard clock to tick around to the hour, when he will open the doors and let the passengers on. A ferry has just arrived from Liverpool, so the queue stretches down the side of the bus.

He sees the back of his own head, less grey than he knows is truthful, his bald spot slightly more hirsute. He is buried in a newspaper. He doesn't read the paper every day, but this memory has decided that he does, and so – he tells his supervisor, the Gardaí, his friends – he was reading the newspaper.

A figure approaches the front of the coach and stares at the windscreen. Darragh shifts under the attention until he realises the person is trying to read the small cardboard sign that lists the stops along the route. He shuffles the paper, squinting in the sunlight that has peaked over the roof of the station building. The glare is so bright the man is just a silhouette as he raises his fingers to trace the letters. They use a frame from the station's CCTV footage for the posters — a fuzzy shot of the stranger walking across the courtyard towards the bus. He is looking down, so the shot is in profile, and his shoulders are hunched forward. In the bottom corner of the image, there is the forecastle of a coach, and through the windscreen Darragh himself is visible — just a blurred suggestion of an arm that could belong to anyone, but he is as sure as sure can be that it is his own.

When he does press the button, right on time, the doors cough open. Two men in shirts with suit jackets over their elbows get straight on, waving their tickets against the reader without stopping their conversation. A woman with a suitcase takes a minute to ease herself up on to the low step, and then Darragh stops paying attention as he doles out tickets and passengers trickle down the aisle. In the memory, he is turned from the door to ease a stone out of his shoe when the last passenger, the silhouetted man, finally gets on the coach, but in truth there could be a hundred reasons why he is looking away. The man asks for a single ticket to a particular village along the northwest coast; he pays with exactly the right amount of money. In his head, Darragh calls out to himself — turn, turn now! look at this man, force out a bit of conversation, listen carefully to his accent, scan his face for scars, his clothing, his hair, check his height, note the shape of his eyebrows, the dirt on his shoes.

Find a detail that you can offer the Gardaí, a clue that will loosen the knot.

But instead, he looks away after the machine spits out the ticket and doesn't look up as the stranger moves down the bus. Then the film skips ahead and melds with a thousand other journeys out of Belfast, down across the border at Enniskillen, through Sligo and on to the dual carriageway, rounding the coast to Westport, and the thirty-odd stops along the way.

All he can remember of this most important passenger is the back of the man's head as he gets off the bus in a seaside village – grey hair, but not white – framed against a red, furious sunset. A slow, painful gait as he stepped down from the bus's ramp. A dark jacket with a collar, white shirt, navy jeans. Swollen knuckles gripping the yellow pole for balance. The other hand pulling a purple backpack out of the luggage rack, slinging it weakly over his shoulders.

And that is it.

In his very first interview, he tried to explain to the sergeant how he has always felt he is standing outside his own memories, rather than a living, breathing participant. But the guard's creased face had had an unhealthy tinge to it, a slight yellowing that screamed, *a man is dead, nobody knows who he is, and you are the least of my problems*, so he had put down the phone all the times he has picked it up to recant and revise his statement. Now, he keeps his story the same, no matter who he tells, even as with each telling the actual experience of it drifts further and further away.

His wife tells him to trust himself, that he couldn't and wouldn't create details like a purple backpack out of thin air, and that he has a knack for remembering things that others forget, like her home phone number from when they had started dating all those years ago, and the fact that his niece likes a certain brand of veggie burgers over all others. She is proud of him, fiercely, maddeningly proud; her love throbs beside him at night and he feels the heat of it every morning, even after all these years.

But at the inquest, in front of the witnesses and doctors and journalists, Darragh hesitates. Then he calls over the guard, who hands him a piece of paper. He is allowed to read from his own statement, exactly the way it was written down in his first interview. It is as if he were reading about a stranger, a stranger who has perfect faith in his own memory.

There was no sign of this backpack on the beach? the coroner asks the previous two witnesses. They shake their heads. He turns to the sergeant. *Has it since been located?*

The guard leans forward, annoyed. *It has not, but our enquiries are continuing.*

Darragh feels his confidence slip away again. He wants to tell them about the comet, about the green-blue light across the sky, about his father cursing, about the hunt through the fields with Simo and wee Andy.

About how he had cleared out the garage for his mother, twenty years later, pulling rusting barbeques and dismembered bicycles out of the back of the shed where the single, dangling bulb didn't reach.

About how, when his fingers had fallen on the stone, it had been rough, not smooth, and when he moved enough of the debris of their lives out of the way and rolled it out into an April rain shower, it hadn't been a mysterious, sparkling-red meteorite at all, but an ordinary chunk of black basalt, and when he put his hand up to it, he felt no heat at all.

the wanderer

The purple backpack is an exclamation mark of colour on the edge of the cliff, the straps sticking out from the insides of the bin like insect wings.

He watches it for a while in case it decides to move. Half an hour later and it is still there, unclaimed. But that doesn't mean much. Yousef has often spent as long and longer in the one spot. This backpack might have its own agenda for the day, or it might be sitting in the bin to shelter from the stifling August sun. He is the type of man who steps around feeding pigeons on the street, so as not to disturb them.

The village is busy, this afternoon, people buzzing past like sandflies. A gaggle of teenagers roar at their own jokes, sitting on the metal tables outside the café. Yousef doesn't pay attention to them and they don't pay attention to him, except to shrink back a little as they pass him. Two boys start a fight and end it again, their voices pitching up and down like swells in shallow water. By the time the sun disappears behind the cliffs, a girl is crying and the rest take turns queuing for oily fish and chips. They roll clumsy attempts at joints and the wafting smoke calls Yousef's attention long enough to remind himself to check for stubbed-out ends once they go away. The café owner, a heavyset woman, emerges to tell them to fuck away off. A boy says something rude to Yousef as they leave and the girls giggle, shoving at each other.

Another few minutes and he is satisfied that the insect wings will not unfurl, that the bag will not take flight. He crosses the empty patch of grass towards the metal bin on the cliffside and pulls it out, lays it flat on the hot tarmac. He taps the bag with his right foot first, and then the left foot, to even it out, but he has to do it twice because the right foot did a stronger tap so two little left-foot taps are needed for balance. And then he has rested his weight on his right leg for too long and needs to transfer it to the other leg again. He shifts a few times, the movements getting smaller and smaller like the last spirals of a dropped coin, until he finally reaches a symmetry he is satisfied with.

By the time the scene has been put to rights he needs to piss, so he shuffles into the alley behind the supermarket. The public toilets are closed; they have been closed since he came to the village, which was not that long ago, really, only long enough for his toenails to grow so thick and crisp that he had to take his penknife to them. Still, he likes it here, in this wild, windy place. The boy in the supermarket leaves out pastries for him at the end of the day, and the chalk drawings he does on the pavements sometimes earn him enough coins for a bottle of vodka. He has pitched his tent in the sand dunes away from the village itself, in a flattened patch of spiky grass between two knolls, and it has been left undisturbed so far, has stood strong against the occasional storm. There is enough of an ebb and flow of strangers, coming out of the lines of clamshell caravans, that nobody seems to notice him.

His piss comes out almost cool compared to the late-evening air. He is sweltering in his jeans and heavy jacket; they are so thick with dried sweat they could stand up and walk away without him. But he does not like to leave anything in his tent during the day; too many times he has come back to a disembowelled pile of canvas and broken metal poles. It is safer to keep things on him, like his penknife, which he sometimes uses to prise open the cockles he finds in rock pools, then roasts in foil over a campfire. But a bag would be best of all, which reminds him to return to the cliffside.

He hooks his boot around the purple straps and gives the body of the backpack a nudge, then quickly retracts it again. The contents squirm with possibilities. There might be a pipe bomb in there; dislodging it will send fistfuls of nails sky high to pierce concrete and metal and flesh. White cars, brown rubble, red skin; the brick walls of the supermarket will crumple and bow, the metal shutters melt away into a silver river. Screams and the time after screams, where there is only running, no breath to waste.

Or the bag might be filled with unwanted kittens. His grandmother had once drowned six kittens in a rain barrel out the back of the farmhouse. She took them, blind and mewling, from the pink and wet space their mother had dug out in the barn. The cat purred and laced its way between her legs as Yousef and his three cousins pleaded with her, promised to rear the kittens themselves, to take milk and bread from their own plates. But she had been as steadfast as the sun – not cruel, but firm, and she smiled sadly at the old she-cat as she let the kittens fall from her arms with a plop! into the rain barrel and laid a slab of wood over the top. Then she picked up the cat and made soothing noises to it, hummed as she shooed the children inside. Now, from inside the bag, he can almost hear the soft scraping of tiny paws swimming endlessly in circles.

Or it could be filled with gold from the Armada, the Spanish galleons that landed here centuries ago, wrecked on a sullen coastline. He read about this in a book that he found on the bus down from Belfast;

the driver said he could take it with him, and he kept it until the pages fell apart in his hands.

Night is falling, a stretched-out, watery sort of night. Loud conversation has begun to spill from the pub on the square. The lights of the café click off, and the buzzing neon sign plinks as it cools. He puts the bag down to investigate the white containers left behind by the teenagers. One is still half-full with curried chips, but the sauce has congealed into a thick orange paste. A camper van roars past him on the road into the caravan park, blaring music from its open windows. In fright, he races across the grass to pick the backpack up with both hands and sits down at one of the empty tables. It tries to float out of his hands, as if it is filled with helium, but he forces it under one armpit. He eases the zip open slowly, and the material sags and yawns forward.

There is no explosion of nails into his eyes. No tiny paws scrabbling towards the widening light, no wet-sodden shapes falling out into little boneless piles. No glint of gold.

———

When the guards take him in, half a year later, they ask what he did with the bag. He finds it hard to pin down the place in time they are concerned about. A hundred, a thousand things have happened since then, all of them important, and he can't pluck out one as being more significant than the other.

They know a man left a purple backpack behind one day last August, the guard tells him, and Yousef was spotted with a similar one. What was in the bag?

He remembers, then, the bag with its straps like insect wings. He tells them about the drowned kittens, the noise of the bombs, the Spanish gold.

The guard tells him to stop acting the maggot, he isn't in the mood for any shite today. Yousef can see that the guard is drifting sideways, slowly, his whole body floating gently towards the far wall of the interview room. But then the room is shifting in the opposite direction, so it cancels the momentum out.

Then a fist is in his face, thumb and fingers flicking together – *pay attention!* He *is* paying attention, to everything, and that is why thinking back to one particular point on one particular day is difficult. He thumbs his penknife, hoping the cold steel will help to pin him down in time. The Armada came centuries ago and broke against a storm, men in metal suits that dragged them down to the bottom of the ocean. The bombs were thirty years or more. His grandmother's kittens, he can't remember. He looks at the wall as he tries to gauge the time from the length of his toenails, flexing and pressing them up against the roof of his boots.

This is a waste of time, says the man.

Yousef thinks the chair he is sitting on is uneven. The four legs do not touch the floor at the same point and he shifts around, scraping the metal legs against the tiles of the interview room. One metal leg falls into the gap between two tiles and makes the unevenness worse so he stands up and paces away to the far wall to put as much distance between himself and the chair as possible.

Sit the fuck down.

Yousef does as he is told and pulls the chair around, but the legs fall in another ridge and the imbalance is worse than ever, and a low, breathy whine starts to come from the very top of his chest, a vibration that is painful against his dry and scratchy throat. He gets up again to adjust it and a pair of hands force his shoulders down. The hands move to the arms of the chair and hold it in place. He cannot see if they are attached to the guard or if they are coming from past or present; all he knows is they are holding him there, his grandmother is pinning his hands to his side to stop him from running out to free the kittens from the rain barrel. The whine begins to pool in the bottom of his mouth and circulate, like a revving engine.

Tell us what you did with the bag. The words come down from behind his head and he tries again to focus on the tether that is connected to the day when he found the bag sticking out – yes, sticking out like an exclamation mark of colour from inside the black bin, straps splayed like insect wings. He knows now – there was nothing in the bag at all; he had even turned it inside out to make sure, checked every pocket and seam. There was writing on the outside, though, stiff white letters, and in a moment he will remember what they said. He opens his mouth to let this out but instead the whine comes roaring up first, like the dark liquid that spits before a fouled tap runs pure.

Then the hands are roving over his body, like cat's paws, roving and patting. *He has a fucking knife!*

And then the table is cold and spit-smeared against his cheek and his hands are a knotted bundle of pain behind his back.

Hours later, in the holding cell, his throat is still scratching with the weight of the words he didn't say. But Yousef knows now that there are no words that will please his captors.

His grandmother taught him to be kind, but she died, screaming, when she invited the soldiers in. She knew, he understood later, exactly what they were there for, the men in their coarse clothes and hard eyes with guns slung over their shoulders. But still, she opened the door to them, sighed and stood back to let them in. He and his cousins watched from the hill above the farmhouse. She sent them there as soon as the roar of jeeps and shouts came over the hills, and they ran, ran fiercely with their heads down. When the fires stopped burning, they stirred through the ashes with long sticks, but there were no bones, not even the small, fine ribs of a cat.

A lifetime has passed since the soldiers came, and he has wandered many miles since, by land and by sea, lived under many roofs, among many people. But there are always those that believe cruelty is the key to force any lock, because it is power they crave, and power is finite: it must be taken from others. The only comfort they offer is the heavy thunk of a plank laid over the roof of a well.

The man who left the empty bag on the cliff had not been one of those men. He had sat beside Yousef for some time, without speaking, sat and watched the world go by. Eventually, the stranger asked about the remains of the wrecked ship on the beach, if it was possible to walk out to it when the tide was low. Yousef didn't know, but he had seen other people making their way across the sand, like little scurrying ants.

The stranger listened, without turning his head, and finally he nodded. *For years I searched*, he said, *and he was sleeping here all along.* He put his hand on Yousef's shoulder, stood, then crossed the road towards the supermarket. He pulled a thick stack of letters from his bag, placed them one by one in the postbox built into the wall; to Yousef, the green slit seemed to swallow them greedily. Then the man pushed the bag into the metal bin on the edge of the cliff and disappeared towards the beach.

The guards did not ask about the stranger, but if they had, Yousef would have told them that he was kind.

There is noise out there: behind the heavy metal door of the holding cell, a conversation is happening. They are arguing about him. Inside the cell, there is only hurting, all over his body; hurting in his hands, his throat, his ribs. He kneels to rock over and back on his shins and begins to hum, a hum to drown out their words. The dark walls drip away and instead his grandmother's farmhouse appears to sway; around him, her humming, as she salves her cat of its loss.

TWO

the seaman

The two men speak to each other in the mess hall in low voices, in Tagalog. When the captain comes into the room, they switch to English so as not to offend him, ramming words together in a random order. But he doesn't seem to notice that what the Filipinos are saying makes no sense. The captain doesn't notice much of what the crew does, another strange thing on this strange ship. Manoy has worked with cruel captains, and kind, and those who fell in between. Captains who had let unpaid wages pile up, and captains who kept the bridge as neat as a pin. A few months ago, he was at sea when the year changed; the captain had invited them all on deck, allowed them one small glass of champagne to toast the new year.

But this captain is as proud and as puffed up as a fighting rooster. Angelo laughs at his shiny shoes that slip on the deck and shirts that are pure, pure white. He is reckless too; he wears an expensive, sparkling wristwatch that he shows off at any opportunity. Manoy once saw a man's hand degloved after his wristwatch got caught in a closing safety hatch. The skin had been stripped off almost whole, and the five fingers hung from the hatch like a bridal glove. The seaman stared at his hand, then at Manoy, and tried to hide the wound behind his back, as if embarrassed by this nudity. Then the man collapsed. They were a hundred miles off the coast of Thailand, so the first-aid officer strapped up the man's fingers and wrapped bandages around it until it looked like he was holding a fistful of candyfloss. Nobody knew what to do with the hand-skin; after a half hour, Manoy eased it – and the watch – into a plastic bag and put it at the back of the freezer room. When they arrived in port to meet the company's agent, the seaman was sent off to hospital in a tuk-tuk, the plastic bag clutched in his good hand. The ship left the port without the injured man, and on time. He sometimes wonders if he kept his hand, if the company gave him a pension. He guesses not; they are masters in many ways – according to their glossy purple branding, their handbooks and leaflets – but excel at placing blame on anyone but themselves. The man who lost his skin probably had to pay the tuk-tuk driver himself.

It is thanks to the company that Manoy is on this vessel in the first place. A harbour pilots' strike in Providence had caused them to miss their connecting voyage, and some underhandedness in the wording of the contracts meant the company were not liable for their lost wages, their accommodation, their transport – for anything, really. Out of their hands, the company said, even though they had already closed their fists. So when a notice was posted in the hostel looking for crew on a frigate for a two-week journey from America to Rotterdam, Angelo had signed them both up – himself as engineer, and Manoy as able-bodied seaman – and they had boarded the ship the very next day.

On the bridge, they shook the captain's hand and listened to his hurried briefing. This was to be a simple voyage; the frigate was returning empty to Rotterdam for repairs, she would be carrying no cargo, so all they had to do was keep the old tub afloat long enough to get there. *Do you understand?* he said again and again, as if Angelo and Manoy were two stupid children. And as soon as the coast fell away, the captain began talking to the white people – the chief officer and Lila, the cook – as if they three were the only ones on board, trying to drive a line between them and the Filipinos. He says *they* and *them* instead of *we* and *us*.

The CO is not so bad. He is Dutch, and he has debts to pay; the company has offered double if the ship comes through on time. If they are on watch together, Manoy can sometimes pull a few words from the Dutchman: a memory, a story, a joke. But if the captain reappears his mouth returns to a slit. Three days in, the CO confesses that the ship shouldn't even have cast off. The port authorities detained her when they discovered a bilge pump that was put on backwards and a score of other safety issues that would cost millions to rectify. That is why they slipped out of port in darkness, because the company wants the ship afloat and would hear no excuses. They plan to reflag her, the Dutchman says, change her name, to hide the broken parts under piles of red tape. It is not the first time that they have hidden damage, injury and worse behind paperwork, and it will not be the last. He hacks and spits yellow as he says this.

Lila is quiet, answering the captain's questions in her Scottish accent with a word or two, tolerating his jokes just long enough to satisfy him, then rolling her eyes behind his back. Manoy likes Lila. It is his first time working with a woman on board, and he is finding her no different to the other galley cooks he has shipped with – same revolting food, same short temper, same attitude to service: take it or leave it. Off the Labrador coast, the waves had rolled so much that Lila produced scrambled eggs for six meals in a row. It is unlucky to sail with a woman on board. But Lila is not a woman in that sense; she is what a woman becomes around men. She is fat, almost defensively so, and her hair is always scraped back into a knot on the top of her head. Manoy imagined a woman on board would cause fights, stir up jealousies, but this is not the case.

It has taken him longer than usual to get accustomed to the ship. It is always an issue for the first few days on a new berth – the stairs are a little steeper, you bang your head on a ceiling that is a little lower – but the disorientation settles after a few shifts. This vessel is different. There is no cargo, so she rides strangely high in the water. He is used to ships that have every scrap of space squared away, shipping containers stacked fifty metres tall, so it is unnerving to see all the emptiness. She is an old ship, with signs in an angular, foreign alphabet, and shows many decades of use. There are raw slabs of deck where things have been removed to make space for containers, leaving behind the faint scent of violence. The outside of the hull is freshly painted, but the internal organs are failing, even if the skin is polished and bright. Angelo cursed the first time he went into the engine room, put his head in his hands.

But there is more than this strangeness: from the very first day Manoy sensed a presence on board with them, and it is this that makes him feel uneasy. It is not an angry spirit, or spiteful, but sometimes he feels something reaching out for him, with grasping hands made out of metal. In certain lights, the walls have the texture of skin stretched tight over bone.

Angelo laughs at him, tells him he has seen ships more cursed than this.

Manoy has spent most of his six years at sea on container ships, hauling slow and steady across endless oceans. He reads the bills of lading sometimes and wonders what the containers might hold. Copper mined in Zambia, children's toys from China, yellowfin tuna from Japan, brand-new Walkmans and VHS players. Hundreds of tonnes of shoes – they say that these are divided into two containers, one for right shoes and one for left, to stop the crew from taking their share, but he has never dared to check. When he closes his eyes to sleep, his body continues on autopilot. Sometimes, Angelo kicks him awake and he is standing in his cabin, waving metal containers into place all along an endless, dreaming deck.

Angelo is older than Manoy's twenty-six by fifteen years, all fifteen of those at sea. He has squeezed along the Suez Canal, seen pirates skipping alongside tankers in the Gulf of Aden, manoeuvred through the firelights of fishing flotillas in Vũng Tàu. But Brazil is his treasure. *São Paulo, that's where the best women are.* Angelo makes thrusting motions with his hips. He often shows off his *bolitas*, a line of spherical implants along the shaft of his penis. The scar is old, the skin healed, but the small bumps look as proud and fresh as new blueberries. *And Filipinos are their favourite. They fuck us for free!*

Manoy rarely visits the brothels; only when they have at least three days of shore leave, which isn't often. He has a wife and a daughter back in his home-town. Gloria knows what it means to have married a sailor; she does not ask how he spends his time in port. She has a big, broad future planned out for them. The first thing she wants is to have another baby, a brother for their precious Celia. Their house is too small for the three of them already, but she has vowed to fill the floor to the roof with children. His parents – and worse, her parents – agree: one child is not nearly enough.

So he must work and work. The pay he brings home is much more than what he would earn in an office in Manila, even if it is less than what the white seamen are paid to do the same job. For Gloria's planned future, he must spend six months at a time at sea – longer, since the pilots' strike – and just three weeks at home. Three weeks to hold little Celia, for her to demonstrate each new thing she has learned in his absence. Each word or action she shows him is a knife in his gut. He wishes he could freeze his daughter in motion, like a wind-up doll, so that she comes to life just as he arrives and walks up the path to the front door. When he closes his eyes at night, he pictures it: the door bursting open, Celia racing down and into his arms, while Gloria beams pride at him from the doorway. But lately, after eleven months away, the picture has grown vague. Lately, all he can see is the shading of his daughter's silhouette behind the glass of the front door.

Too long at sea, and you will break something, Angelo says. You begin to make mistakes. You forget everything you have learned, and you trip over the constant dance of moving parts. *Or something breaks in you*. Angelo knew a man who stabbed another over a kicked bucket of rust remover. Another who jumped from the bridge into the Indian Ocean in the middle of the night. They had to stop the ship, pretend to search for him in the hopeless dark; they told his family he had fallen. Angelo has seen the frozen corpses of cattle floating in the North Sea after a livestock carrier capsized. Angelo has seen a hundred things, and so few of them beautiful. Perhaps the beautiful things are the memories he keeps to himself.

Manoy has lived the same days over and over, skipped others altogether. When the ships cross imaginary lines on the map, time zones shift, stretching or compressing his life. His bedside calendar tells him it is March of 1995 and he has been at sea for almost a year. But he is sure the addition and subtraction of hours means it is less time, or more; he will be paid for less, most certainly, the company will make sure of that. In a few years, the entire century will change, and he wonders if he will feel the new millennium break over his head like the crest of a dirty wave.

Celia turned five last month while he was on a container ship from Liverpool to Halifax. They were passing an island off the coast of Newfoundland and Manoy clung to the port railings, scrabbling for a few bars of reception to make a call from the satellite phone, even though the sea-ice was wrist thick and the containers looked like frosted teeth on a blue-white jaw. After hearing her voice, he came down below with a wind-red nose, but a smile so wide the top of his head could have snapped off.

The company rings every day to check on their progress across the Atlantic, and ask for more speed, demanding that their schedule is met. But even though the ship is empty, there is still not enough crew. Angelo is doing the job of three people, and Manoy estimates his own effort at two and a half. For double pay, it is true, but some nights he wishes he could take two shiny coins and use them to prop his tired eyelids open instead. He has found Angelo sleeping, arms folded, in a corner of the bridge. That the captain has not noticed – or does not care – about his crew's exhaustion, says much. He is a foolish man, who thinks because he is captain he knows better than the rest of them, that he is more important to the smooth running of the ship.

The days stretch onward. There is still work to be done – there is always work, even without cargo – rust-chipping and hosing and oiling and mending and recording and marking. Manoy walks the deck often. There is a twinge in his left knee he is worried about – an old injury where he slipped too early off a ladder and landed square on his kneecap – so he tries to keep active. If he cannot walk, he cannot work, and if he cannot work, he will get nothing. More, he wants to be able to run up that garden path to Celia.

One day, he hears the clang-bang of the anchor line against the hull, even though he knows from the computer on the bridge that it is secured. He follows the sound to the front of the ship, to the small locker where the chain pools, but finds the entrance sealed over with a red iron plate. The seal seems to have been done in a hurry; the welding is rough and uneven. He tries to pull at the inchworm line of fired steel, but his fingers begin to cramp. The sound doesn't stop, exactly, but it fades and changes, becomes softer and less industrial, until he isn't sure if it is just the crashing of the waves against the hull.

There is not much else to do, other than work and walk and work and walk. There is no karaoke machine, even if they had the heart for singing, or even a VCR. For any crew, these things are worth their weight in gold. On his last voyage, somebody bashed up a brand-new cassette so badly it would only whine in the player and show a blank screen. There was a scrap between two crew about it soon after, a bloody nose and a bruised collarbone. The injured man told the captain he smashed it off a wire mesh in the engine room. Back in the olden days, it might have been knives at dawn over a woman, for the sake of a pair of tits. But now it's a closed fist for a cassette and shut up about it after.

So he walks instead. On deck, he feels a stranger's breath on his neck, as if someone is about to tap his shoulder to tell him something. When he tries to sleep, he imagines he hears the anchor line clanging, the sound swelling and fading. He tries to shake the sensations away, like a dog casting off water. Manoy knows his friend is feeling it too, but he will not speak about it.

Hollywood gets into your brain, Angelo tells him, without looking up from his work.

They are six days out of port when the storm comes in.

The wind picks up slowly, but soon they are driving hard into the swell, the bow kicking off dual waves of white foam. Angelo meets Manoy on the bridge as the watch is changing at dawn. The horizon is full of low, bulbous clouds that come closer every minute, darkening the water. Angelo reaches down over the bow, as if his arm could stretch all the way to the surface of the water below.

Like a dog with a bone in her teeth, he says. And to Manoy, it does indeed look like the ship is smiling, mouth clamped upon a white wave.

He feels the squall begin in the heave and twist underneath his feet as he goes downstairs to his cabin. The dance with every ship is different, of course, but you fall into the rhythm. A storm on an unfamiliar ship is something ugly; nothing is where you expect it to be, and on this strange, echoing ship it will be even worse. He straps himself into his bunk to sleep, and he is grateful for the fatigue that pulls him under.

The wind rises and backs around lunchtime, and the ship trips over waves in an uneven shuffle. There is no heavy-weather briefing in the afternoon, and the captain disappears into his cabin again after dinner. Manoy and Angelo look at each other. They have seen the reports on the bridge, the shape of the low-pressure system that is darting towards them.

The pitch and the sway continue all evening, the corkscrewing and slamming. The barometer traces a plummeting line. Manoy passes navigation readings to the CO, who adjusts their course to the south slightly. The waves are now coming side on; the slamming turns into a roll. The phone lights up; it is Angelo, to say the engine room is rolling too, *like a fat whore in a bath*, that he swears an entire winch jumped sideways, and there is a pinprick leak of diesel that he has not found the source of. *Tell him to slow the fuck down*, he roars at Manoy in Tagalog, or *this cunting ship will break apart*.

Manoy switches to English to pass the message on to the CO. As he does, a wave comes in like a punch, right in that soft place under the ribs, and both men stagger a handful of steps. The officer pulls back the throttle, to smooth the way, but a call comes up from the captain's cabin. Manoy does not hear what is said, but the CO takes his hand off the throttle, spits into a corner and winds it back up, until they are making twenty, thirty knots. They fly. Angelo calls from the engine room twice more, but the CO's hand does not twitch.

Manoy's watch continues through twilight, when the waves change from green to orange to black. Off the starboard end of the bridge, a floodlight traces the waves, little explosions of rage and power. The spray coats the windows in a fine mist. The troughs are invisible at night, the ship rising up like a roiling gut and crashing down again. He has never been on a rollercoaster, but he imagines the sensation is the same – your stomach left behind in the air as you skate down the track into infinity. He has promised he will take Celia to Disney World some day.

They reach the eye of the storm around three in the morning. He goes on deck to stretch his bad knee again, to get away from the angry heat of the bridge.

The sky is torn like an ancient sail, and a dusting of stars appears through the rip. Day will not break, but the darkness will slowly ease and lighten.

For now, for now they are alive.

———————

A good storm is a storm you sail out of. And they do sail out of it, while Manoy is sleeping, strapped to his bunk again. The next morning, the sea is flat and cool, like a drunk embarrassed by his antics the night before.

But the ship has not fared so well. They have been forced off course, far north of the English Channel that would take them to Rotterdam. They must turn and sweep down the coast of Ireland. But the route change swallows up more fuel, and Angelo's cursing has reached a constant, feverish stream. The engine clunks and putters. One propellor slows, then speeds up again; the frigate is so long and heavy that it takes a minute for the course to change, and by the time the helm corrects to port or starboard, the propellor has restarted. Their gait is limping, like a dog that has had its pelvis broken by the wheel of a car.

After another heated conversation over the satellite phone, the captain disappears into his cabin, furious, and it is left to the CO to tell the rest of the crew that they must put in for repairs. They must detour, to a small port nearby on the west coast of Ireland, so small it is not even on some of the maps. It is the closest and the cheapest option, and that is what matters most to the company.

On his last night watch before they slip into the channel that will lead them down towards the new port, Manoy goes to check on the wheelhouse. By dawn they should be steaming into the docks. They had meant to make the approach in daylight, but their faltering engine has slowed them down further and they are behind even their worst projections. They all heard the shouting down the phone through the ship's thin walls. Now the captain wants this trip over with; he vows he will be in port by morning and propped up in a bar by noon.

There are a set of maps on the table, detailing the final stage of the detour. They are filled with funny, make-believe names – the Eriador Seamount, the Lorien Knoll, the Porcupine Bank – and then the small, teddy-bear island of Ireland. The maps are pale, fixed relations of the radar screens, where the terrain is constantly updated, where soundings are taken every few seconds and the sea floor mapped like a thief casing an unlocked house.

Manoy is surprised to see the captain on the wheel, but perhaps there is a tricky manoeuvre required that he does not trust to the CO. The speed seems fast for a coastal approach, but the captain is purple-faced and annoyance throbs from him in waves, so he keeps his mouth shut. It takes Manoy a minute to recognise the soft, woody smell coming from a flask on the table. He picks it up and feels the whiskey jostle over and back like a tiny ocean.

He goes out on deck to walk a loop instead, to stretch out his knee again. The air temperature is milder since they hit the warm Atlantic Drift, and the aching is not as bad as it was further north. He hopes it is healing truly this time. The night is not pitch-dark, rather a purple dark that leaves a lush afterglow behind his eyelids. In the deck lights, a pair of birds flit across the stern, over and back. They have trailed the boat since yesterday morning, when a squall sent a confusion of flying fish on to the deck. Angelo made short work of a few of them, and Lila baked them whole for supper. The fresh fish were bland and grey, compared to the battered whiting that fills the freezer, but they convinced each other that they were delicious.

Just before dawn, it starts as a pinprick in the black distance, the suggestion of a blinking eye. Manoy makes another loop of the deck, and by the time he returns to the bow, the blinking light has become a stream. He stops to count, holds his breath, and the shaft of light comes again. Every ten seconds, the twisting arm of the lighthouse beam sweeps out over the water. Next, a tapestry of lights appears, but he isn't certain, at first, that it isn't another passing island. He has never come into a port so small, where the docks haven't been eye-bright and sprawling. He feels a strange tremor in the ship under his hands, as if the sign of land unnerves her.

They are cruising now, fifteen knots, and faster; skipping through the soft water, silent as an albatross. The sky lightens and takes the sting of the beam away, but Manoy's tired eyes still feel like they are painted with grit. Hard lines of land begin to appear, flickering in and out of sight as the clouds flit past them. Off to the north, there is a last free fragment of horizon, a white bank of possibility before the coastline appears and the lines converge.

He feels the presence again, beside him at the forward railing. He is sure now, whoever this spirit was in life, it shows no malice towards him: it is part of the *us* rather than *them*. The two of them cling to the railings like eager children at a fair, facing into the surf.

The lights swim closer, and through Manoy's bloodshot, exhausted eyes, it is not the rugged coast of Ireland that he sees, but his village, his house, his home. His parents are there, and Gloria, and his uncles and aunts and cousins too. Celia is opening the door, racing down the garden path towards him. He urges the ship on – and she feels him, she moves with him, like a lover catching the pitch and thrust of his hips – and together they steam on, into the morning and home.

the cook

At the edge of the village, land meets air meets sea, and a handful of buildings shy away from the cliffside to cradle a half-moon of grass. Early morning rain is misting the windows of the café.

Inside, a woman is moving slowly, bending and straightening, bending and straightening. Her back is hurting. It always hurts. There are days when Lila doesn't acknowledge the pain, and days when she does, but it is always there, a dull ache just above her right hip. She has tried a bouquet of medications, injections directly into the joints, has even had the ends of the nerves burnt away. But still the pain comes every morning, as predictable as the dawn.

A strong jolt, the doctor said, when she finally convinced him to do a scan of her back. Previously, according to him, it had been a pulled muscle, bad posture, stress, anxiety, depression, obesity, the menopause and everything in between. Then, after the scan, it was there on the screen, in black and white – not that she could understand much of what the doctor showed her, pointing out little knobs and indentations along her spine, measuring the degrees of damage. It looked like something belonging to an animal, a piece of viscera left on the side of the road. He had noticed the slackness in her face, her drifting attention, and trailed off. *The injury was probably caused by a strong jolt.* She didn't bother telling him she knew exactly what had caused it; if he couldn't do his own job she wasn't going to do it for him.

Today, like every day, she begins the complicated arrangement of buttons and dials that wakes up the kitchen in the old café where she works alone. Refills the oil in the deep-fat fryers. Wipes down surfaces she knows she wiped down last night. Empties the drip trays from the coffee machine. Counts the bags of frozen chips. Takes slabs of breaded fish out of the freezer to thaw.

The fish is shipped in from abroad, even in a village this close to the sea. Her supplier tells her that these days, it is cheaper to send the fish to China to gut and fillet them, then ship them back to where they started. The sheer waste of it, the convoluted ridiculousness of the whole thing, makes her laugh. The harbour down below the cliff used to be full of trawlers, but there are only the lingering marks of industry: gouges in the concrete piers and buoys that guide the way for nobody at all. The lighthouse, just visible from the café window, struggles to life every evening like an ancient showgirl. Next door, there is an empty bar; a sturdy building, but the green paint is peeling and one of the front windows is broken. The half-finished housing estate where she lives blooms like a horrible fungus on the top of the cliff, the developers long gone bankrupt. The houses are ugly mirrors of each other – narrow, pebble-dashed, with peaked roofs that are at the wrong angle to let the sun flow liquid into the streets – and most of them are empty. The village is being battered by the recession, people tell her, with businesses closing every day and a flood of young people emigrating. But she suspects this place was a lost cause even before that. She has become an expert in lost causes.

The rain is clearing, the sky brightening, and a few cars are appearing. Lila does not bother to flip the sign from closed to open; it rarely aligns with reality. She often decides to lock the door, draw the shutters and sit for a time on one of the hard plastic chairs. Sometimes she finds that her throat is sore, and it is only the rough pain that lets her know she has been silently screaming.

A strong jolt.

In the Hebrides, where she spent the first thirty years of her life, some of the islands are so small that they have billboards that say: SLOW DOWN, THERE HAVE BEEN 7 ACCIDENTS THIS YEAR. They use the word 'accidents' instead of 'fatalities', because road deaths are so rare on the sparsely populated islands. Most larger towns on the mainland tot up the deaths and give an exact annual number, or mark dangerous spots with white crosses to warn other drivers. It shocked her to find that in some cities, car crashes aren't reported at all. They happen so often that they are just a statistic at the end of the month; a lifetime of grief and pain and horror neatly disguised behind percentage points. After the accident, Lila wanted to find every single one of the billboards on the island and mark a bloody '1' across them. One fatality, in a coffin covered with dog-daisies.

It was nobody's fault, the police said. The car her daughter had been a passenger in swerved to avoid a sheep on the road, the left back tyre had skidded in a rain-sodden ditch, and the car had flipped over. Why didn't they run the sheep down? she wanted to ask. Let it fly over the bonnet, squash it flat, reverse over it? Surely a fifteen-year-old was worth more than a sheep, even two, or ten? She was ready to take a knife from the kitchen and slit a hundred, a thousand throats, make a grisly sacrifice to whatever power-drunk gods were out there, if only they would tell her how many sheep would bring her little girl back.

The last thing her daughter's boyfriend remembered was a strong jolt as the tyres dipped into the ditch, and then nothing. He came away from the accident almost unscathed, just a bruise in the shape of his seatbelt. At the wake, she had to half-carry him outside, his arm over her shoulder as he retched and gagged on his grief. The brightly lit house was a shimmering halo behind them as they staggered into the darkness.

A strong jolt.

She was in the galley when they hit the sandbank, arranging things just so for an early breakfast before they left the ship. The impact wasn't sharp, but drawn out and forceful, like the slow grinding of continental plates. Everything in a galley has a magnetic base, to keep it from moving during storms, but there were no magnets in her shoes to hold her in place. The ladles and pots and plates stayed exactly where they were, but she went flying over the worktop, landing spreadeagled among the kiwis, squashing them beneath her bulk.

She knew she had injured her back, then, but in the chaos that followed, she didn't have time to take stock of herself. She struggled up flights of stairs that tilted at a wild angle, kiwi pulp dripping from her chest. She squinted into the misty dawn to see what had happened, trying to understand why they had stopped moving so unexpectedly. When the alarms were silenced, and the captain had stopped screaming, the only sound was the creak and groan of metal twisting against itself. And while the crew – the captain pale with shock, the haggard-looking CO, the two Filipinos muttering to each other in their own language, and Lila with a dull pain in her back – waited for the coastguard's helicopter to winch them safely to shore, the village glittered like a dawn jewel on the cliffside.

First, she had to stick around for the attempts to refloat the ship. For a year or so there was still hope that the damn thing could be relaunched. Crews went out with diggers and tractors every couple of weeks, hoping for a tide high enough to unstick the doomed frigate. The local coastguard teamed up with long-retired fishing trawlers to do the hauling from the sea – the harbourmaster couldn't risk bringing in a larger ship and blocking off the port completely. Not that there was much shipping traffic to block off, as she understood it, but it would have been another black mark against the whole silly event. As it was, the papers had their proverbial field day; they sent reporters out to take pictures of the fractured hull, interviewed the villagers who stood around and watched like dull-eyed cows. When they came to talk to Lila, she slammed the door in their faces. And all the while, the storms and tides were sinking the hull deeper and deeper into the sandbank, swallowing it a little at a time.

Then, she had to stay around for the inquiry, to give an account of what had happened and who was at fault. Had she noticed anything strange before the incident? She didn't know. Had the captain appeared competent? She didn't know. Had the crew mentioned any difficulties or equipment malfunctions? She didn't know. Had the company provided adequate training and support? She didn't know. Did she have anything else to add to her statement? She did not, and the frustration palpable in the harbourmaster's room brightened her mood a little.

Outside the official building, the local guard grunted at her and told her that she could go home now. She stared at him blankly until he walked away, unnerved by the mute, fat lady looking at him with such disinterest. The young, acne-pocked man had seemed flustered from the very first time she met him, waiting for the crew on the cliffside, blinking tiredly in the dawn light, and she didn't blame him. Crashing a ship into the side of a country seemed a crime too big and ridiculous for a small-town copper to even conceive of. What could he do, arrest the ship? The captain? The entire company? An international incident like this was well above his pay grade, and his capabilities; she got the impression that he was as thick and as unctuous as undercooked eggs.

And since then, she has been arguing with the shipping company to approve her sizable medical bills, to compensate her for the fact that she will never work in a galley again. This would be a miracle in itself, she knows, as this particular company is notorious for wriggling out of tight situations. But there is no sense of urgency; since the economy crashed the docks have emptied of traffic, the harbourmaster retired. And there is no cargo for the company to salvage, as the ship had been out of circulation for a number of months. The emptiness, the inquiry suggested in formal language, had affected the height and ballast of the hull, causing the captain to miscalculate the depth of the shipping channel. This, combined with engine-room damage inflicted in the earlier bad weather, was likely the cause of the collision with the sandbank.

But Lila suspects it was just the ship itself that simply gave up; it was falling apart, even before the storm. That they had to do an emergency diversion afterwards was unsurprising: she had heard the engineer arguing with the CO, and she could hear the red screech of frequent alarms even from the galley. Add to that a captain who was an overconfident drunk who shouldn't have been at the helm in the first place, and it was no wonder the ship had foundered.

But the company bailed the captain out, at least, miraculously finding him not at fault. Last she heard, he was a real-estate agent in Connecticut, with his name on bus stops and his own radio jingle. The Dutchman went right back to sea, but the Filipinos slipped away like ghosts. She was a bit sad about that – one of them was a crass, rough bastard, but the younger one had been polite to her, almost deferential. He had spoken often about his daughter – her hair, her favourite foods – in halting English. She hopes he made it home to her, that he wasn't forced into another chok-ing contract on another ship, and another, as the years of her young life drifted by him like icebergs.

She decides to believe that he went home. When she pictures him, with his daughter in his arms, he is smiling.

A strong jolt.

She hadn't meant to go to sea in the first place. Instead, she had taken a cookery training course, over on the mainland, as suggested by her grief counsellor. She did it because she had little else to do, and it pushed out the darkness for one day more. So every morning for six months she took the ferry over, learned to separate eggs, get cakes to rise, the difference between an aromatic and a herb, what vegetables to pair with what meats.

Most of the other people on her course dreamed of having a little restaurant of their own, with candle-sticks and doilies and a specials board that changed every week. Lila never wanted a place of her own. She hadn't really been sure what she wanted, besides a reason to wake up in the mornings. She was never able to drum up much enthusiasm for the food itself, to the frustration of her tutors, who seemed to think this a personal insult. To her, it was fuel, and little else. But she liked the mechanical steps of cooking: a list of steps she could follow and tick off. If you do this, in these proportions, at this temperature, for this long, it will create a meal. If that meal is consumed, it will prolong a life for a number of hours, before becoming shit, which will be pushed out, groaning and stinking, and flushed away.

On the last day of her training course, with her qualification still wet, she had simply stepped on to the ferry to go home to the island, but instead of climbing the stairs to the passenger area on the top deck, she went downwards and walked into the kitchen. They had laughed at first, when they heard what she wanted, then took her on.

But after a year working on the ferry, she itched to get further away. The cargo ships criss-crossing the Atlantic suited her; the menus were even simpler and often she would be left alone in the galley, with no assistants or superiors or stilted conversations. She had respect, when she was in charge; the seamen knew that to upset her would lead to eggshells in the omelettes and steaks that bounced when they hit the floor. She liked to think of the men as little toy figurines that she had to fuel each day, and they, in turn, kept the huge machine running.

After the ship crashed, and she was stranded in the village, she had done the same thing as she had all those years ago – walked into a kitchen and asked for a job. The owner had been an elderly bachelor, with no family he was willing to talk about, and seemed almost relieved to see her. A woman to take over, *to sort things out*, as he said. It was a greasy, grubby place in what passed for the heart of the village. It did breakfasts in the morning and fish and chips in the afternoon; the menu was a faded laminated card that had been stuck to the counter, untouched, for years. The owner seemed to be keeping the place open for the sake of it, because it was what he had always done; there were certainly no raving reviews or customers queuing outside. He was a difficult man, rigid and often rude, and she suspected he had little to fill the hours after the café closed. They rarely spoke about anything except the business: ingredient orders and rat traps and cleaning schedules. He never asked about her life, and she never asked about his.

Then the man had sickened – cancer, the type that men are embarrassed to talk about. Lila sat with him, drove him to his appointments, filled out forms when his hands lost their strength. When he died, the whole village came out for his funeral; it turned out everyone had known him after all, oh, and they were very sorry, very sorry indeed. When she didn't reply, didn't repeat their platitudes back to them, their solemn faces turned sour. Two of his grown-up children appeared out of nowhere, in sleek black suits and sunglasses, to stand at the top of the church and accept handshakes. A grand-child ran up on the altar during the service and tripped, skinned his knee on the coarse carpet and began to bawl. The old priest had to make a rough gesture to get his father to take him outside, and neither man nor child reappeared for the rest of the service.

The next week, a solicitor rang to say that due to the recession, the family were looking to dispose of their father's assets as quickly and straightforwardly as possible, and would she be interested in making an offer for the café. She laughed at the solicitor, told him she would rather buy a dead dog, that it would smell better and cause less trouble.

But that night, she thought about the money she was owed, if the shipping company could ever be persuaded to open their tight fists. As long as there is a chance of squeezing some value out of the ship, she knows she will never see a coin of compensation.

Still, she fell asleep thinking about candlesticks and doilies.

————

A strong jolt.

It is more than a decade since the ship crashed. Her back still hurts, but still she gets up every morning and opens the café. Nobody told her not to, after the owner died, so she saw no reason to stop. She pays the bills, orders ingredients when she runs out, calls the exterminator when she sees mouse droppings in the storeroom. At the end of the day, she turns off the dials, puts the kitchen to sleep. Empties the oil in the deep-fat fryers, wipes down all the surfaces.

Only a few people now remember who she was and how she got there. A woman over the age of fifty is invisible, a fat woman more so. And a fat, middle-aged woman who works in the back kitchen of a takeaway? Sometimes she wakes up in the morning and doesn't even see herself in the mirror. She supposes that should make her unhappy, but it is a relief. Even her Scottish accent has softened with time into something closer to the local twang so as not to draw attention.

There has been a FOR SALE sign in the café's window for a while now. But nobody has money, least of all money for a run-down business in a wet and blustery village on the north-west coast of Ireland. Every second shop is shuttered, or they light up for a few weeks with bright banners of hope and promise and then close again. The bar next door closed down when the owners ran out of money; she would have expected that at least to have been kept afloat on a tide of sheer alcoholic misery.

But sooner or later, someone will buy the café, and she will be forced to leave. It is just a matter of time. But then, her whole life has been waiting. When she left school at fifteen, she was waiting for someone to tell her she couldn't, that she was throwing her life away. After that, she was waiting for someone to fall in love with, someone to sweep her off her feet. When a boy came along who vaguely fit the bill, she jumped in with both feet, arms open, ready to receive. There was a point after her daughter was born, after the bastard fucked off back to the mainland, when she wasn't waiting, when she felt alive, when she could taste and smell and feel clearly. But ever since that sheep stepped out on that road, in front of that car, Lila has been waiting to die.

She watches the wrecked ship from the café's window every day, seeing the tide wash around it, rust climb up its sides, the hull buckle and break. Sometimes she suspects it steered itself into the sandbank, broken and exhausted by whatever years it had spent on the water, whatever weights it had carried, whatever sadness it had soaked up. As metaphors for her life go, it is slightly on the nose, but she will take what she can get. Candlesticks and doilies are not for everyone.

This evening, as she finishes up in the café, there is a sunset redness in the darkening sky. Red sky at night, sailor's delight, but if the weather is fine tomorrow, it will surprise her. It is uniformly grey and miserable, mostly, with sideways rain and low clouds that squat to shit out squall after squall. But when the air is clear, oh! You can see into the past, the future – anywhere but the present.

Then something odd strikes her, and she turns back to the window again. The sunset is coming from the wrong direction, from the south instead of the west. She lifts the counter and steps towards the front door.

Outside, the ocean is on fire.

the firestarter

Distances stretch and compress across the beach as the misting wind sheets sideways off the dunes. A white dot is a discarded buoy from far away, then resolves into the shed porcelain shell of a sea potato. The sun comes out for a few blinding seconds, is swallowed by rain clouds, then bursts out again, dappling the sand into a patchwork carpet of light.

Long-legged sandpipers take flight to avoid the young man walking slowly across the beach, dragging his feet to make black, iodine trenches in the wet sand. A crab skitters out of his path and into a rock pool, holding its claws high like a boxer. Donal aims a steel-capped boot at it, but the water is deeper than it looks; his foot moves sluggishly, as if time underwater is running a few seconds behind. The crab easily avoids his boot, and a slow chill begins to seep through the fraying leather and into his sock.

The sandbank ahead of him stretches almost the length of the beach. When the tide comes in, it looks like the bar of a drowning island, before disappearing entirely under the waves. But today is a neap tide, the lowest of the low, so the shipwreck is fully visible, lodged drunkenly in the sand. Broken metal spars angle into the wind, darker brown and fuzzy with algae where they lap at the water, and the deck railings are curtained with dried seaweed. On the lower, reef-split side, the ship is being eaten by the sandbank itself, all the way up to the deck. The other side is elevated, the portholes crinkled by metal frames into a line of frowning eyes. A seagull starts up from one of the windows, purple-tongued and furious, shrieking at the approaching figure.

Donal follows its flight over his shoulder as it shrinks into a pinprick. Back closer to shore he can see a few people out for an evening walk, despite the uneven patches of rain. A man's braying laugh echoes across the open sand, joined by another, and another. He rummages in his pockets, pulls out a dwindling naggin of vodka, closes his eyes to swallow. When he opens them again, he is blinking in the sudden darkness. The rain clouds have cleared and the setting sun has slipped behind the wrecked ship, making it rear suddenly up from shadow into technicolour.

———

His older sister swears she saw the ship crash, that the ground itself had shaken in a miniature earthquake. The deep bellow of the horn had woken her up early one morning, and as she padded to the window, her bedroom floor jerked sideways with the impact.

Donal was too young to remember it, but still, he doesn't believe her; she lies as easily as other people breathe, to him at least. When he was six, she gave him a stick of chewing gum for the first time. He swallowed it, unknowing, and she shrieked that his insides would glue together, that her friend's cousin had died that way. He spent two days with a strange, hot feeling in his guts, certain that his body was about to seize up like a rusted suit of armour. He refused to eat his lunch in school, and it was only when his teacher rang home that the story came out. Their mum had given them both a smack – her for lying, him for believing it.

Next, his sister told him that Santa Claus watched what he did in the bathroom, and in Donal's head that had become tangled with the crow-dark man who stood on the church altar. That Christmas, he solemnly asked the old priest to bring him a remote-control truck. He got another smack for that, for showing his mother up in front of everyone, but later he found a set of palm-sized die-casts under the Christmas tree. He assigned them personalities based on the arrangements of their grilles and lights, whether the bonnet smirked or frowned, and his father had almost seemed pleased.

At seventeen, he has saved up enough from his part-time job in his uncle's garage to buy a second-hand hatchback, one that has kind, bovine eyes. His father tells him he should be thankful for the job, that the economy is royally fucked and that half the country is on the dole. Donal likes the work: with engines, there is a cause and effect, and problems can be puzzled out with enough time and patience.

But in school, his brain turns numbers into dancing figures, and words never stay still on the page. The other boys in his year talk about emigrating after their final exams, to Sydney and Toronto and San Francisco. They sound like made-up places to Donal, fantasies; he knows he is too thick to ever go with them, to ever have their easy manner, when every interaction feels to him like a complex equation. He has little in common with them – all they want to talk about is the particular anatomy of the girls in the village – so he spends hours driving along the back roads alone.

As a rule, he doesn't believe a word his sister says. But he is finding it harder and harder to disbelieve her when she calls him a useless waste of space. Sometimes, he closes his eyes and presses the accelerator flat against the floor, creeping faster and faster, until the air is roaring past the open windows, roaring in his ears, roaring in his brain. And sometimes, when he looks closely at his car, instead of kind eyes, it seems to have the cruel, angular face of a locust.

———

At the front of the wreck, he steps over a huge, rust-orange anchor that is half-submerged in the sand, the chain leading into a dark hole in the bow. He ducks in through one of the unblocked doorways, shrunk to three-quarter height in the sand and lying at a funhouse angle. Inside, the corridor is too slanted to walk on, but he can balance himself on the slopes between the wall and the floor, crouched into a wide-legged shuffle. Graffiti paints the walls, blocks of bright colour and scrawled names that are faded with the comings and goings of the tide. He takes a left, a right, finds a closed door and pulls vaguely at the wheel-shaped handle, but it will not budge. Another corridor, another blockage; his thighs are beginning to cramp from his squatting position.

The ship's innards have been gutted by scavengers, both human and animal, anything of value long removed. But he has come to look for the engine room, for the heart of the leviathan. He saw the tide retreating as he looped the village in his car, the ship rearing dry, and decided to walk out to it in the absence of anything else to do on a Friday evening. He wonders how big the engine will be, if it will fill an entire room. He wants to test the crankshaft and trace the pistons with his fingers; if he can see how it works, it will be one small thing in this world that he does understand.

Finally, a stairwell opens out into a large area at the very front of the ship. Half of the space is under the sandbank; the floor tilts upwards and the metal roof has collapsed in one corner, creating a spout that funnels the wind down and through the ship's intestines. The creaking whistle is uneven, in and out; a congested smoker's breath. He squeezes over a slippery lump of rubber, climbs up a slope of ripped-out lino until he can stand upright and rolls his neck around in a wide, slow circle.

The last of the sunlight leaks through rusted holes in the hull, like stage lights on a watery runway, spotlighting the remains of a soldered-shut hatch. Curious, he finds the metal leg of a broken table, shoves it under the corner of the hatch to use as a lever. The iron seal shifts a little on one side, but no matter how he hauls, the metal covering will not budge further, and he drops the table-bar in frustration. His hands are rusted red from its coating; he dips them into a puddle and wipes them against his trousers. The water swirls with a thin film of orange.

When he straightens, the vodka hits his bladder like a punch. He goes in the corner; it takes a while for the flow to start but a patter-patter of urine marks a map out of dried salt. Some rubble shifts in the dark, and he is surprised at the jolt of animal dread in his stomach, surprised and then annoyed at his own fright.

He folds himself back into his jeans with both hands and starts to shiver; his clothes are still wet from the rain and his leaking boot seems stuffed with ice. He bends and tosses a few pieces of debris aside, finds the wooden frame of the table. A clump of dried bladderwrack stretches down from a half-open door like an unfurled tongue. He tears it to confetti, the sharp edges of the blisters leaving red lines on his fingers. Tips out the remains of his vodka on to the shredded pile, fumbles an ancient lighter out of his jacket pocket and lights it, pushing the wooden scraps over the weak flame.

He turns back, aims a desperate kick at the hatch, and it shifts a little further. He kicks again, forcing the steel caps of his boots into the space where the metal has lifted away from the floor. It grinds open a fraction more – *come on* – *to fuck* – *come ON* – he needs something to show for this rancid piss of a Friday night, when his peers are likely at a party without him, his sister is laughing at him, his mother is shaking her head in disappointment – harder with each kick, and still the crack is not wide enough for him to get his fingers under. He's panting now, with exertion and loneliness; his collar is too tight and there's a hitch of a cry in the deep triangle between his lungs. He rests his elbows on the sloped wall, puts his head in his hands and closes his eyes. The flames behind him send a gentle warmth trickling down his neck.

Slowly, he realises that the steady whistle of the ship has been joined by a percussive rumble. The sound is uneven enough that it could be the accidental hum of the wind through distant pipes, starting and stopping again – but for a moment, just a moment, it sounds like someone is speaking, singing even, in a language he can't understand.

Then, from the hatch in the corner, a dark patch breaks away from the shadows and moves, undulating against the reddened hull. The silhouette has its arm raised, as if it is desperately reaching for something, for anything. Donal whimpers, scrabbling away from it. Then the dread smashes into the alcohol in his blood, like soldiers against a shield-wall, and flips over into rage. Some sad bastard has been watching him all along, watching him piss, has heard him crying over nothing at all.

He stumbles across the rubble, fists clenched and raised, but he slips on a pile of seaweed that has the texture of wet jelly. He lands on his back, hard, so hard that his teeth snap down on his own tongue; he tastes iron and is winded for a gasping, frozen moment. The floor is angled so the blood dribbling from his mouth seeps backwards towards his nose, and it's in his eyes, his fucking eyes. He tries to blink the redness away, force air back into his lungs, haul himself to his feet, but panic and shame have him now and his breaths are short, panting gunshots. He elbows his eyes to clear them, to triangulate the distance between the intruder and the doorway, to find the way out.

But there are only shadows twisting in the flames, and no sound except the wind and the crackle of salt-light. The campfire has spilled over a little and is still going, flames green-licked from the salt, and the damp in the air is turning to steam. Pieces of broken wood collapse in on themselves and a shower of sparks screams against the metal. They race up strips of dry seaweed to the ceiling, where they settle into flames that ripple in upside-down waves. His brain kicks in to tell him that metal does not burn, and he starts to breathe again, but there is a flicker of bright light and a flowering of intense heat that forces his eyes closed.

His feet come awake without consulting his brain, so he is already racing to the hull when the flash of damp flame hits him, kicking and kicking with his steel-capped boots at the salt-weakened metal until it gives way, and he's bending now and heaving at the small opening with his hands, shaking his jacket off and over his fingers to protect them, but the thin leather shreds to pieces almost as easily as his bare skin. Light and heat and noise; he's reaching through the sharp hole in the hull, reaching towards the clean air, his shoulders slanted and wiggling, his hips, his knees stuttering over the jagged edges of the opening, hands palm down into a pool of water, being shat out, reborn – and then he's out, he's out! slopping head and shoulders first into the water like a seal, twisting on to his back to look back at the ship, panting.

The fire is hidden now, the yellow glow contained behind the metal hull. There is a shudder as something falls inside; a greasy bang and a whomp of flame billows upwards. He pulls himself out of the water and lurches to his feet, then goes down again, over the thick links of the anchor line that rises and disappears into the white-hot hull. His hands are destroyed, flaps of skin are hanging from his fingers and blood is outlining the lines in his palms.

From the distant beach floats a scream, a shout, but in the darkness the voices are disembodied, unreal, coming from a world away. He slaps himself to stop the shaking, spits syrupy blood from his bruised tongue. His limp turns into a stagger, into a run, away from the billowing flames, away and back to his car, away home, just away, and he doesn't look back until the memory of heat has faded from his shoulders.

the diver

At high tide, it is simply a bare patch of ocean about five hundred metres from the shore. The only hint that anything lies underneath is a slight cross-hatching of the waves, a rippling patch that runs perpendicular to the rest. Otherwise, the water is calm, although the sky threatens rain; the distant mountains are fading into mist.

The three men stare at the surface in silence. Finally, the boatman clears his throat, looks over at Robert and his silent partner. *Well, are you going in?*

There's always a moment, just when he dips his head below the water, when Robert is convinced that he is going to die. His body rebels against going under, convinced it is suicide, and it takes a firm grasp of logic to persuade it otherwise.

He's seen this dread descend on others, from novice divers to veterans. A primal reflex just takes over and screams: *air, I need air.* They rip the mask and mouthpiece from their face, ignore the air tank on their back and kick out for the surface, forgetting anything and everything that they've learned. The air is that way, their animal brain says, and off they go. If they're lucky, they choose the right direction. If they're lucky, they have enough air in their lungs to make it to the surface. If they're lucky, they aren't deep enough for compression sickness to set in. If they aren't, they're fucked. Afterwards, the reports will say they *got into difficulty*, as if the diver were stuck on a tricky problem in a maths exam. Drowning due to the onset of an unnameable, unknowable dread doesn't have the same ring to it.

Robert has had to dump weight belts in his time, when things have gone wrong, and has had to break for the surface when his spare regulator clogged up. But he has never felt the blind panic take over. Although the decompression stop can feel like the longest few minutes in existence: just staring at the surface, willing the nitrogen in your blood to dissolve faster so you can get back to the real world, where

Homo sapiens can take the helm again, away from the half-lit underwater reality where you are never sure if you are dreaming.

Robert has been diving for twenty-odd years. When he tells people that he is a diver, their faces brighten. They picture coral reefs, mottled octopuses, tropical parrotfish and David Attenborough voiceovers; they tell him all about their wonderful dives in the Maldives, the Canaries, the Great Barrier Reef. But he is not that kind of diver, he tells them. His business is industrial: construction, maintenance, inspection and repairs. Their mouths sour and turn downwards in disgust when he tells them about the raw sewage, the confined spaces, the sores around his lips from the mouthpiece. The full hazmat suits for dives where the silt and debris are so thick he can barely make out his hand in front of his face, and he has to rely on his groping fingers to free the snag, unkink the pipe, fix the seal. Sitting for hours in a decompression chamber; hosing the toxic waste off with jets so strong they leave bruises.

But I'm sure your dives were lovely too, he says and they usually change the subject.

———

They bring him over from London to inspect the old ship about two years after the fire. The site is near a flyspeck village on a sandbank that dries out at low tide, but the access window is small and the surveyors have struggled to cross the wet sand. The shipping company wants everything recorded, the extent of the damage on file for the insurance, but there has been delay after delay. So far, they haven't been able to photograph the entire vessel, and someone has decided that the site is better accessed by water, at high tide, which Robert agrees with – floating through tight spaces is easier than climbing or crawling.

His work has brought him to many strange sites all around the world, but an underwater arson investigation is a new one to him. Not that it is much of a mystery: from what he has gathered, the guards believe the owners set the fire themselves, to wash their hands of the wreck and claim the insurance payments. Robert himself suspects that local kids were pissing around setting fires and it got out of hand. He did the same when he was a teenager: broke into derelict places, made bonfires out of pallets, drank warm beers and kissed girls, scattered like spiders when the guards arrived with searchlights to break them up. His older brother Stewie had a silver tongue and always managed to talk his way out of trouble, some fantastical tale that conveniently absolved him of all guilt. Robert didn't have the imagination to lie.

But today, it is not his job to prove malice, just to record the site with the camera strapped to his forehead. He's not sure what they'll do with the footage – likely there is some specialist out there who can deconstruct an explosion, turn back the clock, reassemble the pieces. He and another commercial diver – you never, ever dive alone – have been sent to this beach in the middle of nowhere. At the deserted pier, they met a man with an inflatable boat who drove them the short distance to the site, where they are now staring at the water.

Air tank, buoyancy jacket, weights; he spits into his facemask to keep it from fogging up. He signals his readiness to the other diver, a sullen man who seems to have little interest in making conversation. Robert lets the weight of the tank pull him backwards into the water, the outline of the boat shrinking, as if he has heaved himself off a cliff and time has slowed to let him watch his own demise. The water is not deep, though, so after a few seconds he reaches the sea floor, flips over on to his stomach and fins strenuously for a few metres to warm himself up. His thick drysuit keeps out the worst of the chill, but the Atlantic never warms enough for his liking, and the rubber seals around his wrists are a frozen border.

His buddy follows him down to the seabed and hovers a few metres behind him as they fin towards the site. Visibility is poor and a strong tide makes the seaweed stretch and undulate across the rippled sand. The ship looks like it has been lying for a century rather than just a decade and a half – the cargo holds haven't been breached, but the funnels and railings have collapsed, and the entire forward hull is gaping wide open on one side. Robert knows well enough not to go into small spaces where he could be trapped, or brush against anything that looks unstable, but the constant ebb and flow of the tide have cleared out most of the debris. What is left is a shell, the internal structures mostly disintegrated.

The two divers circle the site, slowly and deliberately, their headtorches painting lightning patterns against the hull. On the flight over, Robert studied the map of the ship provided by the shipping company until he could trace his way through it with his eyes closed. Of course, the damage makes the map a fantasy, but he can at least use it to roughly orient himself. They are searching for the ignition point, to confirm what is already known – the fire was set in the forward hull, below the partly drained engine room. The leftover fuel ignited and the explosion came from there.

They drift, Robert rotating on to his back to turn his head in a 360-degree circle, letting his camera capture as much as possible. He checks his watch. The dive computer tells him he has been under for thirteen minutes; at this shallow depth, a decompression stop is not strictly necessary, but the watch face calculates it automatically for him. He reaches for the gauge around his waist and checks it out of habit; his breathing is slow and controlled, so there is plenty of air remaining. He flips on to his back and signals to his buddy with his fist and fingers, and the other man responds with his own reading.

He turns forward again and sees a beige-grey pattern that is slightly offset from the rippled seabed. As he fins closer, the cuttlefish gives up its camouflage and darts across his path. Robert kicks hard to follow it for a few moments, but it finds a pile of rocks and squeezes into a hole no wider than the circumference of his thumb, disappearing entirely. He drifts with the underwater tide, waiting for his buddy to catch up, waiting to catch his breath.

Robert's older brother, the one with the silver tongue, once found a cuttlebone on a white-sand beach in Cornwall when they were children. The thick, leaf-shaped husk was long as their forearms. Stewie gasped when he saw it and announced that it was the soul of a drowned man. From then on, every time Robert went to the beach he glued his eyes to the debris thrown up by the receding tide, hoping to find a soul of his very own. Every glint of white sent his heart leaping, but it was always a razor clam, a piece of ceramic, a plastic spoon. It became a mythical quest for a treasure as rare and precious as a unicorn's horn.

He was a grown man before he saw another cuttlebone, but it was in a book this time, and he learned it wasn't a soul, or even a shell, rather an internal shell that lets a cuttlefish float. He wanted to study marine biology, once upon a lifetime ago, but he didn't have the brains for the science of it, or the patience for the slow and detailed work. He spent years in the civil service instead, doing slow and detailed work that he had even less patience for, and diving at the weekends. Living for those brief submergements, where the only sound was the gentle in and out of his own breath, the whisk-whisk of underwater shoals, the fizzing of photosynthesising corals, the clicking of stones rolling along the seabed.

It was his wife who suggested he quit and retrain; after her third miscarriage their grief became too large for the house they lived in together. His brother, ever the storyteller, had danced around their lives with a lightness of foot until he found a story that swallowed him whole: a wicked witch of an ex-girlfriend who bottled him so hard he lost a chunk of his brain and went blind. Now Stewie lives in an assisted living facility, asks after their non-existent children and pisses himself daily. Robert's wife visits him every weekend, brings chocolate and sports magazines that she reads aloud. She has stopped asking her husband to come along. She knows the sight of his own brother revolts him, and that makes Robert loathe himself even more. These days, he chases the quiet of the submerged. It is only underwater that the voices in his own head stop berating him, as if even they are holding their breath, unwilling to distract him.

It has been years since he looked into Stewie's blue-blind eyes. Years since his brother lay unconscious on the kitchen floor, bleeding and dying, before his stupid bitch of a girlfriend finally called the paramedics. And a lifetime since two skinny boys found a cuttlebone on a white-washed beach.

Twenty-seven minutes into the dive and the other diver signals that half of his tank has been used up. Robert has a little more, but he nods and makes a twirling motion with his finger, turning them both around. The beam from the other man's torch dances like a candle flame. They have reached the very fore of the vessel and there are black streak marks all along the hull where the metal has sweated and buckled. One structure has kept its vague shape: the anchor locker, from what he remembers from the blueprints. The covering over the opening seems newer than the rest of the metal surrounding it, as if it were a later addition. The outer frame is swollen, like an infected boil, but in the centre, it has protruded outwards and burst into a red-bellied flower, petals of metal curling back on themselves.

The opening is about as wide as his hips, and dark; the water changing colour slightly, as if the inside and outside were two different substances, mercury that has sunk under water. The gap is too small for him to fit comfortably into – he is a large man, made larger by the air tank and buoyancy jacket – but he pulls himself along the hull until he can aim his headtorch and camera into the locker. Inside, there are the remains of an anchor chain, barely visible through the silt. This part of the ship is less discoloured than the rest, even allowing for the fire, as if it had been sealed away for years. The heat must have caused the hatch covering to buckle and burst, opening up the room again to the elements.

There is a flash of movement, a glint of bleached bone, and he leans forward to see better, hoping to glimpse the cuttlefish again. He dips his head into the pool of mercury, and suddenly his suit is too tight. He can feel every centimetre of it pressing against his skin, the weight of the thick fabric like a full-body gag. The hood is constricting the blood to his head, his buoyancy jacket is pressing against his lungs, tight, tight, tight, and the water around him is as thick as treacle. He tries to fin backwards, but his buddy is in the way; they flail at each other to separate themselves, but at this point Robert has lost all control over his body and his brain. Panic, sheer panic lands his fist against the other man's head, connecting with a low thunk that is audible even under the water. His mask is clouded with steam; all he can see is grey metal, all around him in every direction as he hurtles away through the silt that his fins have kicked up.

The husk of the ship is collapsing, condensing in on him; he will be caught under the debris and remain there for a hundred, thousand, million years, until he is compressed as tightly as the heart of a neutron star.

———

What the fuck's wrong with you, the boat driver is roaring at him, the engine whining like an angry wasp.

Robert hauls himself over the rim of the inflatable, the blast of pure adrenaline launching him up like a submerged buoy. He shoves away the boatman's helping arms, fumbles with the straps on his scuba kit. A click and release: the jacket slides off him and the heavy tank crushes his foot, but the pain is a bright spark, real, alive. He is alive. He is alive. He is alive.

A minute later his buddy surfaces, spitting out his mouthpiece to curse, and it is only then that Robert realises he left the other man behind, skipped his decompression stop, broke all the rules he has religiously followed throughout his career. His chest is still heaving, but free from his jacket and air tank the awful claustrophobia is lifting. He pulls at his drysuit too, ripping the skin on his fingers against the zip when it doesn't come quickly, peeling his arms out one by one. He breathes deeply, takes massive, gulping breaths, until he is so full of precious, glorious air he could drift upwards off the rim of the boat and into the sky like a lost balloon.

The boatman shoves him aside to help the other diver on board, but Robert hardly notices. The terror is dissipating now, in the dull grey daylight, where the possible and impossible are sharply divided, unlike the underwater world, where all things remain in limbo. But again and again, he comes back to it: his brother, floating below the lip of the submerged hatch, reaching out an arm to him in the shrouds of his blindness, reaching out from the anchor locker, from the bloodied kitchen floor.

Tears are pricking, pushing, flowing from his eyes, dissolving into the rain that has begun to spit from the sky. His chest is heaving again, with grief rather than fear this time; with loss, with regret, with promises to his future self. The others are still cursing, and Robert starts to apologise, to explain away the panic. His buddy's face softens once he begins to understand – all divers know how it can happen, no matter your experience – although he hawks a glob of salty mucous in Robert's direction.

We got enough, Robert says, picking up his camera from where it fell into the bilges. *Enough*.

The boatman shrugs, kicks the engine into forward gear. A squall has settled in while they were underwater, the clouds dropping and darkening, white horses frothing towards them. As they pick up speed, Robert tries to remember what Stewie's favourite chocolate bar is. He will grab a selection at the airport, just in case, and magazines, and he will hold his brother's hand tightly and remind him of the time they found a drowned soul on a white Cornwall shore.

The boat skips from crest to crest as each drop of thick, oily rain bursts on his forehead like a tiny universe exploding.

the artist

The sharp morning light is slanting over the café's rooftop, streaming downwards to refract off the metal tables before launching itself back into the sky. A woman is sitting at one of them, going over a thick sheaf of sketches as a tortoiseshell cat suns itself at her feet. There are a handful of other customers waiting to be served, but the café's owner has stopped to inspect the drawings.

Rhea is trying to explain the scene, to explain why the memory has stuck with her all these years, but it is clear the older woman doesn't grasp the weight of it. Lila has a way of shaping her lips into a downward purse, raising her eyebrows and tilting her head to one side, as if looking at a performing rat. This brusque attitude is refreshing, most of the time; she speaks as cleanly and clearly as a sheet of glass. But today, there is something venomous in her narrowed eyes.

What a stupid thing to remember. Her finger lands squarely in the centre of a sketch, smearing the soft, dark pencil. She disappears indoors again to serve a customer, leaving the sting of her words behind.

The minute she arrived in the village, Rhea was desperate to leave again.

She hadn't meant to stay for very long anyway; she had just picked a random point on the map to catch her breath after the sharp slap of the divorce. Her ex-husband sneered at her plans, and she hadn't been able to disagree with him: she was a terrible mother for leaving her son, an unnatural monster. But she had been drowning alive back in West Virginia, hollowed out, running on less than empty, so she got her things together and left. The drive down from the airport had been grey and dull, with endless raindrops bursting against the windscreen. As soon as she sat down in her horrible rented bungalow – the cheapest and shittiest she could find the island over, in a half-empty housing estate that stank of powdered concrete – she burst into tears. She went to bed with no plan other than to keep running, as far and as fast as she could.

But after a few days, something felt strange about moving further east, further away from her young son. Her little estate looked out on the bay, and she could pretend that she could almost see him, just beyond the horizon. She found herself looking west, often in the mornings, as the dawn travelled over the ocean and through time zones, imagining Mitchell still asleep, snatching a few more minutes in bed before school began.

And slowly, her guilt and shame had eased, and just as slowly, she had fallen in love with this small place, where the sunsets smear themselves across the sky and drown themselves in the temperamental sea, where the clouds skate across her windows like a stop-motion film.

Sometimes, when she is feeling melancholy, she thinks she would've fallen in love with the first place she set foot in, unchained from the schedules and neuroticism that defined her marriage, whether it was a Siberian wasteland or an arid desert. When she told her ex-husband she was staying in Ireland, he didn't *say* anything, of course, but his way of not saying anything is very particular; you can see the silent words spelled out in huge red letters. As if another argument about the breakdown of their marriage would have helped, who did what at what time, the precise chronology of mutual affairs.

Would one infidelity have happened without the other? Do the degrees of closeness make a difference: their son's baseball coach versus a stranger at a bar? Rhea's was the stranger, even though he hadn't seemed like that after half an hour. She never saw him again after that night, when she went out looking to destroy her own life, but she could still pick him out of a line-up.

People always say *it's the eyes*, as if they are some magic portal that lets you see into a person's soul. But in reality, eyes are all variations on a theme – brown, green, blue, creased, folded, popping – and they start to repeat after a while. It's silhouettes that are unique – the shadow a person casts, what they look like behind a window, the shape they make against the backdrop of the landscape. When she teaches, she always tells her students to put a vague figure somewhere off in the distance. The vagueness is the point; the outline has to be generic enough that the person viewing the painting can insert themselves in the scene, dive into the frozen moment.

Rhea half-jokingly calls herself a space–time artist. Because it's that extra dimension she tries to bring to the canvas – both flattening and expanding at the same time; billows of memory in thick furls of paint; the raging fires of loss and the banked coals of loneliness; the sting of a bitten lip and the coolness of an indifferent touch. And then sometimes she decides that all this florid language seems ridiculous, a pretentious charade, when she lets it loose here, in this wild and raw place.

The painting of the ship on fire had sat in a pocket of her brain for years, churning and baking, even appearing in the backdrop of her dreams. She had tried to put a shape on it, but every time she sketched the outline in pencil, the result seemed too flat and soft to capture the truth of it.

When the ship burned, she had been newly arrived to the village, too nervous to even go to the super-market on her own, living off dry pasta and biscuits she had brought from the States. One evening, she stepped out for some air and found half the village gathered along the cliffside overlooking the beach. They were mostly silent, with the odd gasp or cheer, and nobody seemed to mind her joining to watch the flames. She didn't know who called the fire brigade, but when the truck arrived it sat there like a useless slug. The sand was too unsteady to support the weight, the firefighters argued, and what was the point? The arsonist was likely long gone, the ship was abandoned, derelict, and the tide was on its way in. Later, she heard that the wreck was a nuisance, a public eyesore, which might have explained the lack of urgency.

The sun had only just set and the fire was glorious, a smouldering coal against the greying sky. Darker smoke billowed off the heart of the wreck and the breeze took it towards the crowd, in over the shallow water of the incoming tide. The flames were hypnotic, throbbing, as if they were the pulse of a living creature. She sank deep into herself and all noise and feeling faded away, until it was just her and the fire, the fire and her, two points on a flattened plane.

And then she saw a shape come staggering out of the creeping surf. She raised her finger to point, to scream a warning, but there was a clank and a whoosh. *The fuel!* someone gasped beside her as a fireball rose up and out, devouring the front of the ship. When the white-heat faded, the silhouette was gone.

She had been having problems with her eyesight, blurs that came and went, strangely shaped indents in her field of vision. A weight when she moved her eyes, like she was pulling an entire train carriage with her pupils. So she told herself it was another phantom, and stayed watching the boat smoulder until it was full dark and the tide covered it completely. When the last hiss of the flames died away, the crowd broke up, until Rhea was the only one left standing on the cliff.

The next day, at low tide, the firefighters went out and raked through the wreckage. If they found anything – or anyone – she never heard a word about it.

Shortly after that, her fingers began to ache, and the first waves of tingling swept over her. Her diagnosis came slowly, in dribs and drabs, narrowing down like a laser from space, pushing other possibilities aside. Two different doctors told her it was early menopause and gave her brightly coloured booklets to take home. It took another year of scans and lumbar punctures before they could definitively say that it was multiple sclerosis.

Multiples of what? she asked the neurologist, trying to make her voice light and breezy. He had gone into an explanation about glial scars, but she wasn't listening; she was counting the floral tiles on the ceiling, making sure the shapes repeated evenly. When she closed her eyes, the pattern stayed imprinted on her eyelids.

She had just extended her lease with her disinterested landlord, begun her own quiet renovations and been hired to give a series of art classes for adults in the local community centre. She felt more joy in guiding students' brushstrokes than in her own, and she told herself she was too busy to focus on her own work. The truth was that her well of inspiration had drained, and refilled itself with fear, a gentle terror that would settle over her every time she sat down in front of a blank canvas.

Then her son finished high school and announced that he was applying for a diploma in computer science in the city an hour up the road from her. She had laughed down the phone at him, not realising he was serious. He swore blind it had nothing to do with her illness, that he just wanted a change. Then his father came on the phone and announced that the baseball coach was pregnant, a fact he brought up with an icy casualness, and on foot of this she had agreed to let her son come live with her.

He arrived in the late summer with one backpack and she scolded him for his parsimony. They drove to the city and bought two weeks' worth of socks and underwear, and a pair of plaid pyjamas. He started college the week after, and every day he came home with his face flushed with newness. He got a part-time job in the supermarket in the centre of the village, after lying about his experience stacking shelves, and seemed to her to be happy.

In the first weeks after her son moved in, they sat up late talking over endless cups of tea. They didn't talk about their personal lives – he was just eighteen, after all, and still adjusting to a strange new land, and Rhea was awkward and unsure of herself, as if motherhood had been a rubber band stretched across the Atlantic Ocean, and, suddenly released, was still trying to settle on a new shape. But they talked about everything else in the world – their opinions on everything from horror movies to the best way to cut a sandwich – and realised that, in another life, they could have been friends.

Once, Rhea told him about the night of the fire, about the silent, watching crowd, about the heat and smoke that came in waves from the ocean. He walked out to the remains of the ship the next day at low tide. She had pleaded fatigue that was all too real, instead of having to face the long trek over unsteady ground. He came back with some pictures for her, of the gutted iron lumps rusted green against the sunset, almost unrecognisable as a ship, with a dictionary of graffiti that seemed to be refreshed every tide.

And, over the next few weeks, she began to pick up her pencils again. The sketches came to life, in thick and fine lines, as if the memory had needed time and retelling in order to temper itself. Laying the first daubs of oil paint on the canvas felt like letting a ripe strawberry burst in her mouth. It is still unfinished – her hands are weak and tire easily, despite the cocktail of medications she takes daily – but she is pleased with the form it is taking.

The paint leaping off the canvas, so thick and tactile a blind person might read an essay from it. The beach, vast and swirling, as if it is coming out of a dream. The ship, black as black can be, with shape-shifting flames reaching out and into the horizon.

And a slim, barely-there finger of burnt umber, a lick of the brush, suggesting the shape of a watching figure.

Sitting outside the café, Rhea folds and refolds her papers, the tremble in her hands making the sheets dance. She is almost finished the painting; these sketches are the last dregs of memory that she can squeeze from her brain before she lays them out on canvas. *What a stupid thing to remember.*

When she first arrived, almost panting with loneliness, Lila had ignored her attempts at conversation, despite the fact that they were near-neighbours. But Rhea sensed an ache in the other woman that rhymed with her own, so she returned to the café every morning, claimed a table looking out at the bay and sketched over coffee and scones. Often, the café was closed – not empty; she could see a silhouette moving around inside, just closed to the outside world. But she persisted, trying to craft a friendship out of pure stubbornness, and eventually the other woman began to soften.

Now, she can feel a hot rage welling up inside her, like jam coming to the boil. She wants to push over the table, punch the stupid, dumpy woman, kick the cat under her feet into the sun. Lila doesn't understand what is contained in each of her paintings, the compressed time, the emotion; that her dismissal is an accusation of failure, a waste of finite materials; that she is a lagoon, cut off from replenishment—

And then her thoughts float away from her, and she cannot remember at all why she was so angry. It is a ridiculous anger, coming from nowhere, going nowhere. The form and meaning of it is already falling away, and her temper is swinging back and downwards.

She worries that the fiery pulse of her highs and the deep troughs of her lows are something her son has inherited, like knobbly knees and an aversion to cilantro. An artistic temperament, as her husband had sneered at her. Mitchell has never had an aptitude for art, to her disappointment, but growing up he sometimes sent her stories he had written at school. They were unpolished and raw, but there was potential there, a sense of scratching at a locked door. Because a heart as full as her son's needs a pressure valve, a way to release what he soaks up from the world around him.

Her son has never once resented her for leaving him behind, and for that she owes him a debt she can never repay. But she can't find a way to line up her sadness with his sadness; they are two train tracks diverging into the horizon, unable to reach each other. He had to testify in an inquest for an accidental death a few months ago, which shook him – shook her too, if she's honest, the idea that Mitchell could have been involved at all, even as a witness. She will force him to go back to college, back to the States, if that will make him happier, back to his dad and the baby, away from a life as her carer. She will manage, as she has always managed. Her symptoms can flare and fade, with years in between. Today she has walked the short distance to the café, next week she may need the aid of her wheelchair, and she will manage then too. Still, the possibility of her son's absence is already pressing down on her, like fingers on a swollen, throbbing spine.

She takes a sip of her coffee, leans back and finds the rage has become something else, shifted seamlessly into another gear, and it is homesickness, the hot searing lack of a place that doesn't exist any more: her father's pipe in the backyard; a five-year-old Mitchell perched in a tree; the sound of her husband laughing at one of her mother's jokes and warblers in the trees; the dusky, jagged skyline of the Blue Ridge Mountains.

Lila comes back outside, and, instead of sweeping past to another customer, she hovers over the table, picking at the skin around her fingernails. Rhea can tell she regrets her earlier comment, but her pride will not let her say so. She has a feeling that her friend's words were not for her, but trace something older, more personal.

Most of my memories are stupid, she teases, to let Lila know that her slight has glanced off and away like a salmon twisting off a rock. *Tell one of yours instead.* She expects the other woman to snort and shake her head, but a silence broadens between them instead. Outside the bar next door, the owner is rolling empty kegs towards the road, each clatter and curse a punctuation mark against the low susurration of other people's conversation. The noise wakes the cat and it begins to flex and knead its claws against the grass.

Then Lila sits down at the table. She begins to speak, haltingly, of a scene, as polished and perfect as a piece of sea glass: her daughter is six years old, making dog-daisy chains in the back garden, the grass as high as her knees. Her long blonde hair is whipping in the wind, the sun is setting and the chimes over the door are clinking. The flower stems keep breaking – her daughter has weak nails – and Lila has to split them for her with a pin. But not all at once; she brings the dog-daisies to her mother on the porch one at a time, furious all over again with each split stem, and Lila is laughing at her frustration. A shaggy pony snorts over the garden wall at them, drawn by the shrieks and laughter, and when the chain is done, the little girl drapes it around its neck in a solemn coronation.

Rhea does not dare to stir her coffee, to clear her throat, to move, for fear of interrupting whatever stray current is allowing the other woman to speak more honestly than she ever has before.

But she is gone, and it all fades a little more every year, Lila trails off. Her crossed hands convulse in her lap, as if she were squeezing the juice from two peaches.

There is quiet, for just a few seconds more, and then the sky lights up with noise: a flock of barnacle geese swoops low over their heads, keening and whooping. The two women track them with their eyes as they circle around the beachfront and head out to sea. The barman has paused, a keg between his thighs, to watch the geese too. He raises a hand to them, tries to invite them to share a moment of wonder, but they do not notice his gesture, and he returns to his work.

I will paint it for you, Rhea decides suddenly. *You'll sit with me and describe the colour of the sky, the pile of dog-daisies, the snorting pony; the exact colour of your daughter's hair, how she hunched her shoulders, how her fingers moved.* She hesitates, self-conscious once more of her own pompous notions, of putting herself forward like this, intruding on the other woman's grief. *Would you like that?*

Lila nods once, a downward jerk. She does not reach out across the low stone table, but her right wrist twitches as if she would like to.

Rhea smiles. She sees the other woman clearly now. *I will paint your daughter, and the daisies, and there, at the centre of it all, I will put you.*

The tortoiseshell cat wends its way between the two women's legs, making the shape of infinity, and its gentle purring brings something like equilibrium.

the barman

It was just called Murphy's when he took it over, the same as a hundred thousand other places in this strange little country that is obsessed with dead men. The estate agent hadn't known who Murphy was, or if the man had ever even existed. The woman seemed surprised that Matías had asked, rifling through her files, trying to find an answer that wasn't there. The place closed during the recession, she said, reading from her notes, and had been empty ever since. Securely maintained, of course, with regular upkeep, she added hastily, as nothing had yet been signed.

Matías didn't believe this in the slightest. Perched on a corner at the end of the village, Murphy's bar was three rooms and an overgrown garden, with a small bungalow attached to it. The building was painted a greenish colour, with a faded sign and a large, splintered front window that faced west. But the view of the sea was partly blocked by a housing estate, and the café next door filled the air with a thin film of grease. It was a far cry from the blue-sky promotional photos, the rooms stretched by a fish-angle lens. From what he could see, *regular upkeep* amounted to a pre-viewing lick with a vacuum and a polish of the tables. And outside was no better – grey skies, grey rain, grey pavements. A miserable husk of a building on a miserable rock in a miserable country.

It'll do, Matías said, and signed the pieces of paper that made him the owner of a bar on the north-west coast of Ireland.

———

He never expected to follow in the footsteps of his grandfather, as crooked and winding as they had been. The old man's bar wasn't even really a bar, just an open area of the *finca* with a corrugated roof, a few extra fridges and a clay-board for *tejo*. Some days, men came in from the hot, grassy plains in overloaded jeeps, wearing uniforms with the yellow-red-blue stripes of the Colombian flag on their shoulders. His grandfather had handed out loose cigarettes and beer bottles with a lightness of touch, and let these men play *tejo* for free.

When the jeeps came to the farm, Matías and his younger sister Yesica were always sent to do some chore, or straight to bed, even if the sun was still shining. The men wore guns over their shoulders like handbags, black and shiny as beetles. When they got drunk, the children could smell the gunpowder snap of the *tejo* as it thunked into the clay, and hear arguments from their bedroom window.

When he was ten, their family had moved up the mountains closer to Bogotá, away from his grandfather's farm. And when he was sixteen, his father told him it would be better if he fucked off, just disappeared, stopped breaking his poor mother's heart. Whether he was to die in a back alley or just disappear somewhere out of sight didn't seem to matter to his father. So Matías found a man on a prehistoric message board who was willing to pay for a sixteen-year-old Colombian boy to come to America. He took the free tickets, kissed Yesica goodbye and was on the plane before his father knew he had left. When he arrived in LAX airport, he had walked straight past the sign with his name on it – being held by a man who was *much* fatter and greyer than he'd looked in his photographs – and out into the Los Angeles sunshine.

For the first few days, Matías felt guilty, but he was too happy to care. A friend of a friend got him a job clearing tables in a bar, and a narrow bed above a Mexican-themed restaurant. He had to wear a sombrero that made his forehead itch, but he smiled under his painted-on moustache every evening. Five years later, he had worked his way up to junior manager when that same friend reported from home that his sister was pregnant. He had laughed and laughed and laughed. Little Yesica, always clinging to their mother's skirt, now a mother herself at the tender age of fifteen? He was sure their father would kick her out the door so fast her ass would catch fire. But his parents had mellowed, it seemed, in the years since he left. Or, more likely, a teenage pregnancy was a much more acceptably Catholic scandal than a homosexual son.

By the time he gathered the courage to get in touch with his sister, Yesica was a qualified solicitor in Bogotá, a grown woman as fierce as the sun, and her own son was a baby no longer. It turned out it had been Yesica herself who put her foot down and refused to leave; she always had a stubborn streak as wide as a river. She told her brother how she had insisted on taking her high-school exams, and was offered a full scholarship to a law programme. She got the bus up and down the winding, mountainous roads to the university each day, and worked in their parents' shop at weekends. Matías felt positively lazy when she described it to him. The previous decade of his life had involved hard drugs in Berlin, a breakdown in Thailand, a year-long romance in St Petersburg, of all places, and a mercifully short stint at a desk job in Lisbon.

They would be visiting him in California soon, Yesica announced; she hoped he hadn't let his hair grow too long. Then she hung up. To his amazement, he became *Tío Matí* almost overnight. A sister and a nephew – a family – regained with a suddenness that left him reeling.

———

When Yesica called with the news that their *abuelo* had died, she had been firm and sure of her words. Yes, he had gone peacefully in the end; yes, their mother was upset but relieved; no, he shouldn't come home – he hadn't really been considering it; it had been a knee-jerk response.

The first surprise was the inheritance. Where the money could have come from, they had no idea, until Yesica remembered the men with their beetle-black guns who came in from the plains in jeeps. *The old dog*, they agreed.

The second surprise was the size of his share. When he hung up the phone, he sat for a time and tried to summon up his grandfather's face. He hadn't even known the man particularly well. Matías was only one among a flood of grandchildren, and when they moved closer to Bogotá, they only returned to the farm at Easter and Christmas. The man was almost a stranger – why had he picked his grandson out for such largesse?

Then, when he closed his eyes in bed that night, a memory came to him, with such searing vividness and clarity he couldn't believe he had ever forgotten it. It was his grandmother's birthday. They had killed a bird to make *sancocho*, and it had been simmering with plantain and yucca in a metal pot on top of a fire pit. Matías was eight and had gone off all meat, which made his father furious, for no reason he could decipher at the time. His grandfather spotted him slyly feeding lumps of chicken from his plate to the dog, and had chuckled.

His father had come out of the farmhouse then, calling for a leg or a wing, claiming his pussy son would eat the whole bird if it killed him. His grandfather had shushed his son-in-law, whose mouth turned into a hard line before he stalked away with his hands in the air. Then, the old man pulled the chicken's carcass from the pot and twisted it around so its back legs were facing upwards. He dipped his machete in the flames and let it heat there for a moment, then slid it into the belly, angling it to slice away a lump of meat. The ovaries had cooked in the heat of the stew, and the unlaid eggs descended in size from golf balls to peas, surrounded by a thin film of flesh. He popped one out from under its covering and offered it to the boy.

Here, he said, try the eggs instead.

In Matías's mind, the old man is huge, his face crease-lined, squinting in the sun despite his wide-brimmed hat. His hands are as wide as shovels, and the egg steams in the humid air as he drops it into the child's palm. His mouth waters, remembering the savoury, crumbling bite of the orange yolk, and he hears again the whisk-whisk of the machete as his grandfather wandered off through the long grass.

Now, in his memory, he is shocked by the heat that comes streaming out of the old man's silhouette as he walks away, as if he is a dark wound in the world made especially for love to come through. The offering of the eggs – an outstretched hand, an opening, another way – and his eyes cocked a little to the side; as if he was seeing his grandson for the very first time, looking at him and him alone, not simply as a branching of his mother and father and sister and a score of other blood connections.

That is the last clear memory he has of him. But obviously, something in the old man had sustained itself for thirty years, some itch had gone unscratched, and the result was enough *pesos* to retire on, waiting in a bank account with his name on it.

Don't ask me, Matí, Yesica sighed on the phone. *I think he was gone a bit caca in the end.*

———

When the money finally came through, Matías had played with a few ridiculous ideas for almost a year, feeling that an unexpected windfall should be used for something just as unexpected. Then an article popped up online, a jokey one with lots of exclamation marks – Would You Like To Own This Pub In Ireland – and he had thought to himself, *yes*, I would like that.

He was nearing forty and had been sick of Los Angeles and the denseness of people, sick of hot places and of shielding his eyes in the sun. He found himself dreaming of the green, landlocked seas of his childhood, the grass-plains that undulated in the wind. Yesica argued that a cold, wet rock on the Atlantic Ocean was a poor substitute, but the idea already had its claws in him. So he quit his job, bought a bar, and moved to Ireland. Three Simple Steps To Change Your Life.

Horrified at himself, he got drunk on decades-old Irish whiskey the day after he got the keys to Murphy's and fell asleep in the middle of the musty barroom: a nightmare of paisley wallpaper, red leather seats and mouldy carpets. He woke the next day to a crippling hangover and an equal amount of regret, which morphed into a resolution to throw money at the place until it went away. Then he could go back to mixing cocktails in the sun.

But somewhere along the way the regret had softened and turned into something lighter, something almost hopeful. He found himself singing as he stripped wallpaper and polished furniture. Sleeping better in the freezing bungalow behind the bar than he ever had in his life. Driving around the country to search through second-hand shops, collecting pieces of kitsch. After spending most of his life on the move, the idea of decorating his own place was intoxicating, and he regularly filled his battered van to the brim. Even when the bathrooms had to be replumbed, it felt like an annoying pinch rather than a slap.

The owner of the café next door, a burly middle-aged woman, had watched the renovations with suspicion. When he waved at her, she grimaced. *Welcome to paradise*, she said sarcastically, and went back inside. A few of the village elders had walked by while the place was under renovation, trying to reminisce about good old times spent in Murphy's. None of them knew who Murphy was – or, at least, they all had a different origin story for the man, the myth, the legend. His favourite was that Murphy had been a sailor who took deathly ill while on shore leave, but the captain insisted the ship sail with the tide, so the crew buried him with a loaf of bread and a shovel – just in case he woke up.

When Matías told the passers-by he was thinking about changing the name, they had seemed put out: an expression of confusion paired with a tilted head and a grim smile. One woman even blessed herself as she walked away. At first, he couldn't read these strange Irish people, the way their faces did something different to their words, the way their sentences were the wrong way around. *Hah?* they said, just *hah?*

As if all the infinite possible questions in the universe were contained in those three letters. And then *ah!* with an upwards jerk of the head and an inhalation, which could describe anything from a stubbed toe to a tsunami to a lottery win. They thought he, the foreigner, was irredeemably stupid, of course, but they slapped him on the back all the same and went away shaking their heads.

Of course, there had been the obligatory *faggot* screamed across his front window in red paint one morning, but for a boy used to his father's ire, this was barely a prickle. It had upset other people more than him, and when his freshly repaired front window was broken, he kept it quiet, deciding a quick clean-up was easier than another round of outrage. The local priest had condemned the incident from the pulpit, and he was plagued by people stopping by to shake his hand for a week. Bemused, he only figured it out when Oona – the old woman who had blessed herself – mentioned the priest's sermon in passing. Matías was surprised by this, remembering his father's fervent grip on his rosary, his devotion to La Virgen that didn't seem to soften his fists.

Oona has a sort of spidery influence – knows everybody, everything, and manages to rarely pay for her own drinks. She has given him many a history lesson from the bar stool, as if it is her duty to educate him on the generations of people who have lived in the village: the intricate webs of marriages and variations in the spelling of surnames, children who have become lawyers or writers or butchers or statistics.

Every speck of land on every continent has as much history, he wants to tell her. He has been all over the world, stayed in bedsits and campsites and penthouse apartments, and every one of them has a backstory as rich. More, where people are wedged together like sheets of paper: in the cities, every neighbourhood is its own universe, every inch of space is layered with lives, with memories – arguments, spilled food, bird shit, blood, sweat and tears – so thick that they waft up like the steam off his grandfather's pot of *sancocho*.

You have to find the eggs, he wants to tell this pot-bellied woman, who teeters on the bar stool like a bucket of paint. *Those are the real treasures.* But that's not a discussion Oona would understand, or welcome, so instead he smiles and nods. And the old woman releases her words of wisdom like air bubbles from an underwater clam.

But all the same, this strange sort of welcome from the village's most venerable one made him feel more at home than a hundred shamrock-headed leaflets from the bank. And as soon as he reopened, the regulars trickled back in – shaking their heads at the decor, poking at each item like curious kittens – but still, they came. So, as a compromise, he kept the pub's name, but added to it – Matí Murphy's.

Donal arrived into his life one day when his beloved van had refused to start. He was supposed to pick up Yesica and her son from the airport and had spent the week previous arranging and rearranging the furniture in the guest bedroom, suddenly terrified that he would disappoint his visitors, that they would sneer at how small and condensed his life had become.

Oona was passing by – she is permanently passing by; he is convinced she does loops of the village looking for something to poke her nose into – and recommended he call a particular mechanic. She named him as car magician and engine whisperer wrapped into one. From the description, he was expecting a middle-aged man, but Donal was in his early thirties, tall and lean, with silvery scars on his hands. He had a gentle manner about him that disguised a slight nervousness, and spoke mostly to the engine instead of Matías himself. But whatever magic Donal had in his ragged fingers wasn't enough to save the old van. Instead, he offered to drive him to the airport in his own car. All the way there they spoke sparingly, but the silences were comfortable, full and easy, like the feeling after finishing a good meal.

When Yesica arrived, glamorously dishevelled after the flight, she assumed this to be her brother's boyfriend, and kissed him on both cheeks. Donal went bright red at being accosted by this Colombian whirlwind, but recovered in time to shake her son's hand. The car journey back was noisier, Yesica bombarding her brother with questions and advice in a flurry of Spanish, and Matías was surprised to find himself annoyed at her, missing the gentle silence of the journey up. When they got back, the visitors disappeared inside while he apologised for his sister's expansive personality.

I get on with my own sister like a house on fire, Donal said. *There's lots of screaming and running away.* It took a beat for his nervous joke to register, but then they both laughed, their eyes meeting properly for the first time. Matías asked to buy him a drink as a thank you.

After he left, Yesica leaned on the bar and examined her nails. *I think you should keep him, Matí.*

Two years on, Yesica's son has two *tíos*, and they share the bungalow behind the bar with an obnoxious tortoiseshell cat. The space is small, but Matías still scours the markets and second-hand shops every weekend. The bar itself is groaning with artefacts he has picked up – a diver's helmet, a stuffed mongoose wearing a tie, a life-size cut-out of Dolly Parton, a farting toilet seat, two phrenology busts. Donal has instituted a one-in, one-out policy to prevent the walls from buckling under the weight of this tat.

So when he sees a leaflet outside the supermarket advertising a craft fair, he isn't planning to buy anything new. He goes along to the community centre to show support; he is a pillar of said community now, even if Oona is the only one who thinks so. Most of the stalls don't entice him – he has had his fill of handmade jewellery, personalised fridge magnets, seaweed soaps – and he is almost relieved to be leaving empty-handed. But on his way out, a large canvas catches his eye, a dreamlike mess of heavy paint and whorls. In it, he recognises the curve of the landscape, the westerly crag of the cliffs and, in the middle, a bright billow of steel-rimmed flames. The ship had burned long before he arrived in the village. Now, from the clifftop path, it is little more than a few rusting chunks of metal that appear at low tide. He would never have guessed it used to be a ship; he assumed the lumps to be another one of the markers that lined the old shipping channel until Oona told him what it was during one of her speculation sessions about the the body found on the beach last summer.

Matías doesn't understand how this one mystery has such a hold on this community. Corpses show up all the time, and most of them stay anonymous. He saw his first on the street when he was seven, an indigenous woman who was curled up in a doorway. *Don't look*, his father said, stepping over her. It took three days for the woman to be taken away. He supposes that the dead man on the beach has drifted into myth, a fireside story, alongside Murphy, buried with a loaf of bread and a shovel.

The squiggled name at the bottom of the painting is unfamiliar to him, although he vaguely recognises the artist when he asks about the painting: a dandelion of a woman in a wheelchair. He shakes her hand and they make pleasantries – she is American, and he tells her about his time in LA – and they commiserate over the cold winter nights they have been having. She confides that she has only recently begun painting again and that it feels like she is lifting her skirt and showing the village her dirty knickers. He tells her that she can always turn them inside out to get another day's wear out of them. The depth and loudness of her laugh startles him.

She shakes her head when he points out the painting he wants – he suspects the extravagant price was an attempt to dissuade buyers – but brightens when he tells her that he owns Murphy's and wants to put it over the bar. He leaves with the painting, wrapped carefully in brown paper, and an invitation to coffee at the café next week. Even though it is just next door, he has never really spoken to the owner, after her sarcastic welcome, which doesn't surprise her. *A difficult woman*, she sighs. *But give her a lever and she could move the sun.*

When he gets home, he wipes the painting's frame down with a damp cloth and leaves it outside to dry as he goes inside to assess the few remaining patches of empty space on the walls. Across the street, Matías's new van is parked beside a vintage sports car with a curved bonnet and cheerful headlights. Donal emerges from their home next door, keys in hand; the car is his latest project, and most days he disappears under the bonnet for hours at a time. He slows as his gaze falls on the canvas, but he is in the middle of the road before he manages to stop completely and come back.

Matías sees this through the large front window of the bar and comes out to see what the matter is. When he gets outside, the look on Donal's face is strange, jerking, as if he is a record that is skipping on the same lyrics over and over again. His groping hands find a bench, and he sits down in front of the frame to stare at it, reaches out a finger to touch a lick of paint in the foreground of the scene. Behind him, the cat is trying to force the netting on an old lobster pot open, snuffling at the memory of fish.

Matías looks at the painting and back at his partner – this gentle man who wakes up with terrible bed hair, has a habit of falling asleep in the cinema, who could burn a glass of water, who he is planning to ask to marry him – and he is suddenly a stranger, a pulsing cloud of acidic dread. He grabs his shoulder and shakes it. *What? What is it?*

Donal stares at his silvery-scarred hands, and then his fingers clench, digging dark, uneven trenches in the skin of his face. Then he swallows, forcing shards of himself back into a whole. When he opens his mouth, his words are pulled from some awful, hollow place.

THREE

the widow

She cries like a terrible ocean when they show her the pictures of the dead man. The French police told her that it was probably her husband, but still, the shock of seeing his purple-splotched face, even in a photo, hits her somewhere beneath her ribs.

The police station has a low ceiling and the white wall paint is pocked with bubbles. Ancient fingers have pressed into the paint to burst the protrusions, exposing the grey, powdery plaster beneath. The Irish guard is kind; he brings Monique strong tea and biscuits: two ginger nuts wrapped in plastic. She has never had ginger nuts before and the kick and fire of them is a surprise. He is fat, with yellowy hair and old acne scars. He reminds her of her dead son, although his eyes are blue where her son's were brown.

The officer brings her husband's things, all wrapped up in little packages, and an inventory list that he reads off in a dull, formal tone. Monique has to nod at each item they extract from cellophane and lay out in front of her, acknowledge it as belonging to her husband. The items he places on the table are boring, mostly: some clothes and a pair of boots, nothing that hugely interests her. But when he sets out the wedding ring, she tries it on immediately to see how it feels. It is too big for her finger and she puts her tongue through the gap between the gold and her skin. The guard looks at her strangely and Monique takes the ring from her mouth, lets another wave of sorrow spill out over her lips.

The guard rests his hand on her shoulder then, in sympathy. They are all very, very sorry for her loss. He says that her husband was buried by the council almost a year ago in a cemetery outside the village, in a ceremony attended by four guards and a grave-digger. The headstone doesn't have his name on it, but she can have it engraved now, if that is what she wants. Or she can contact the embassy and try to take the body home, bring her husband back to Poland where he can lie beside her family.

But going back is not part of her plans: she likes it here in Ireland. The distances between things, by bus or by train, are short and sharp, enough to lull her into a doze but not a deep sleep. When she sleeps deeply, the blackness behind her eyes transforms into swirls of colour that dance and cross-hatch against each other. And then they turn jagged and things begin to rise up and shape themselves, not into faces or memories but impressions: of closing doors and musical notes that start out high and pure, then flatten and spread out like the prongs of a rake.

But she does not tell the fat guard any of that. She doesn't tell him much of anything; for now, it suits her to not speak very much English. They had wanted to bring a translator, but she shook her head; she can understand well enough when she wants to, her mind is just clouded by grief. They are very understanding. But there will be formalities, the guard says, they will need to confirm his identity, ask her some questions about her husband, how he ended up in Ireland, fill out all the official paperwork. But they have a name now, something to go on: Thomas Meyer.

I don't mind telling you I'm relieved, the guard says, *to finally put an end to this mystery*. He grins, and then feels ashamed for grinning when she wells up again. He coughs awkwardly and keeps his hand on her shoulder as she cries and clutches the photograph she has brought, a faded image of her and Thomas in the Berlin sunshine all those years ago.

She first saw his face on a programme after the main evening news at a bus stop in Strasbourg. There were three televisions sitting underneath the departure boards. Two on the outside had been set to a weather report and a golf tournament, but the one in the centre was showing a list of people with active police alerts, and it was there that she saw him.

They had done something to undo his deadness: propped open his eyes and brought blood back to his cheeks, using some kind of trick. His face moved from side to side, his eyes opened and closed, but still, she could tell he was dead because the stench of it seeped through the layers of distortion and wafted out from the screen. When they showed a version mocked up with a heavy, silver beard, Monique gasped in recognition, and heads turned towards her. She stood and pointed at the screen – *où est-ce?* she demanded of no one in particular, and she had to repeat it twice more before somebody answered her.

C'est Irelande, said a young man who was waiting on the same connection as her. Before he spoke, he wrapped his foot securely around the loop of his luggage, as if he expected her to grab it and run away.

Mon mari, my husband, was all she could say.

The young boy yapped to the security guard at the loading bay and he yapped to someone else on the phone, and there was yapping all over like small dogs barking at her feet. They took her to a cold room and showed her the photograph from the television again, and again she said, *mine, mine, mine.*

The French police did not like the look of her clothes or the bags that she clasped with both hands. *Vous connaissez cette personne?* said one of them, refusing to meet her eyes, disbelief colouring his words.

Oui. His name is Thomas Meyer and he is my husband. What has been done to him?

There were more phone calls then and more yapping and more questions, from foreigners this time, and she answered them as best she could. Her English isn't as strong as her French, but it suited her for it to seem weaker than it is. They wanted proof, proof that she did indeed know this man, before they took it any further.

The building where Monique was living was close to the police station; she wanted to walk, but the bastards took her elbows and drove her there anyway. It took some time to find what she was looking for, because her things were laid out in identical brown boxes, and the photographs were in unorganised loaves spanning decades. There were her dead son's things too – old shirts and a pair of football boots, notebooks and car magazines – and a cat that strode through it all like a queen, hissing every time a pile was dislodged.

Désolé, désolé, she apologised, without meaning it. The police waited in the kitchen while she went from box to box searching for a photograph to show them. She heard one of them taking a glass from the cupboard and washing it quietly before filling it with water, embarrassed by being embarrassed.

Finally she produced the photo she had been looking for: the one where Thomas has his arm around her and she is young and smiling. He has an iron-grey beard and his fingers have dented the cloth on her shoulder a little bit, all four of them curved around into a tight grip, but he is smiling and she is smiling, and when she showed it to the policemen, they looked at their own files and then they smiled too.

She fell asleep in the unmarked car they drove to the airport in. They took her through a special access gate, through a queue made up of just herself. She laughed as she stretched out her arms as wide as they could go to fill up the space where the people had been taken away.

The police didn't come with her on the plane, but that was all right, because she found a woman to speak to instead. In broken English she explained that she had finally found her husband, that he had been lost for a long time, and she had been waiting years to close the coffin in her heart. The woman took her mask off after a few minutes to hear better, and when she had finished the woman wiped away a tear, crossed her hands over her chest and repeated Monique's words to herself: *the coffin in your heart.*

The guard allows her to bring the wedding band back to the hotel they have booked for her. They will interview her again in the morning, when she is feeling up to it. She leaves the station and gets straight on a bus. She sleeps, a light and easy sleep, and the driver wakes her up at the end of the line with gentle hands. She waits for the next bus and takes it somewhere else, and at the end of the day she is in a city on a river. She books into a room under a different name, tells everyone she meets about the coffin in her heart.

When the fat guard finds her again, he is upset with her for some reason. He wants to know who she really is. She tells him, but that makes him worse; he wants a different answer. She tries out a few options, but none of them please him either. He takes her back to the room with the low roof and the bubbling walls in the rear of his car, a long, juddering drive that makes it hard to sleep.

There is no tea this time, just water, and when Monique asks for ginger-nut biscuits the guard ignores her. *You look like my poor dead son*, she tries to tell him, to make him understand. She switches to French but it is no help. The guard begins to walk in circles around the table. He puts down a file in front of her, and there is a picture of her face, and some words in a language that she decides not to recognise.

He says nonsense words: the photograph she showed them was a lie, that the man with his arm around her is a theatre actor named Thomas Meyer, someone she met in the street after a play, and who – despite a passing resemblance to the dead man – is alive and well. They have checked out her story, and she has never had a husband at all. They have found her son, who isn't dead but lives in Poland, and he is worried about her because she is a compulsive liar with a history of *psychiatric events*.

How can you hear anything when you yap so much? she asks him.

He becomes angry then, so angry he slams his fist into the table and spills her glass of water. He makes phone calls, says, *we're right back to square one, square fucking one*. He turns to look at her and his eyes are scrunched up like shiny, furious buttons.

They give her a place to sleep for the night, with a rough blanket and a soft pillow. But she knows that there are heavy and broken things waiting for her when she closes her eyes. So she wraps the blanket around her and runs her nails along the wall until it is daylight. The next day there are more people, a woman who tries to take her hand and tell her she has rights. Her eyes are bleary from staying awake, and she wants to get on a bus or into a car so she can sleep. They give her a cup of tea, but still no biscuits.

They are being very lenient, the fat guard says. Her son has pleaded her case at the highest levels, and even though the tabloids and internet mob are out for blood, they have decided not to prosecute her for wasting police resources. The best thing for her is home, family and a secure environment, the woman says kindly. So, it will be more travelling, back to the airport, and on to a plane to Warsaw this time, where, she is told, her son is waiting to take her home. The other guard throws his hands into the air and leaves the room as the kind woman talks and talks and talks.

Yap yap yap. Small dogs bark the loudest. But she knows that if you catch them just right with your boot, between the ribcage and the belly, you can launch them up and away from you. Your foot will break some precious part in their body and they will lie there, panting. Sometimes they get up and sometimes they don't, but they never bark at you again.

She cries when they take the ring off her. She still tastes it on her tongue.

the guard

In the facial reconstruction, the dead man's eyes are open. The forensic technicians took the blue-white face from the morgue, tinted it yellow and purple and pink, poured artificial blood back through channels long closed off. Forced its eyes open, added a wet sheen; even animated it, so the face could move around, blink and yawn. It is lifelike in a lifeless way, a puppet that is perfectly, artfully carved, but without that Pinocchio spark.

Gavin saw the body, on the beach that morning. If the corpse was a radiator, it was still plinking and cooling, fluid still trickling through its pipes. But it was definitely a human thing, an animal thing – this digital creation is a thing of machines. The sergeant is not old enough to feel so uncomfortable with this technology: halfway through his fifties, even if he does feel like he is ageing at an exponential rate these days. But these sophisticated tools make him uneasy. Others in the force cheer every time a crime is solved through some strange new tyranny of science. And then Gavin sits in court, watching abusers and thieves and rapists walk away, because the evidence wasn't there, the jury wasn't convinced. Motive, means and opportunity aren't enough any more: if a suspect *really* did it, they think, there would be some log of it in an overarching filing cabinet. Some great algorithm in the sky should have been watching, recording – a microscopic sliver of DNA left behind, an internet search for getaway cars, a selfie with the prone body. If there is no such evidence shown in court, well, it's the guards' fault for not finding it. And so, the criminals walk away, free, not gloating – most are smart enough to wait until they leave the steps of the court behind before bursting into cheers and high fives – but still free, struck out, dismissed. And there is no justice.

Justice is a name we put on a certain set of outcomes, his first lecturer in criminology had said, *but it isn't a finite quantity.* You can't hand it out like parking passes. Say a man beats his wife so hard she loses their unborn baby. A woman left permanently scarred, a child that will never see the light of day. What would be a just punishment for that? A fine? Imprisonment? The death penalty? Ask a hundred people and you'll get a hundred answers. There is no sentence that will perfectly fit every crime, and even if there was – so what? Could each person live their life as they wished, crashing and burning and maiming and stealing, if only they take their allotted punishment afterwards? Our justice system isn't the confession box. There is no wiping the slate clean, because how could we possibly quantify a future that will never exist, because *this* crime has been committed, in *this* place?

Sometimes we have to settle for half-clean, the professor said. *And sometimes that slate just stays dirty.*

A man lies dead on the beach on a summer's day. Start again from there.

The witness who found the body was certain he had drowned. It wasn't the first time the Gardaí had been called down to a report of a body washed up on the rocks, although that seems to happen more often in winter than summer; such accidents are more frequent when the sky begins to darken after lunchtime and the days are only as long as a yawn. Only they aren't called *accidents* any more, now that there is no fear of the Church turning them away from the graveyard – another little cruelty to add to the historic pile. But the way that the man's body had come out of the ocean looked too neat for the circumstances, and his clothes were bone dry besides.

First, they needed to find out who he was. They did the usual appeals for information, rang hospitals, hotels, homeless charities, everywhere they could think of. It quickly became clear that the man wasn't a local, or even a visiting tourist. The village was heaving with people all out to chase the rare summer sun, but there was no report of a missing father, brother, grandfather. He had his contacts in the capital go through their missing-person records, then reached out to Scotland Yard and Interpol and beyond. For the first few weeks, every time the phone rang, he was sure it would be a grieving wife, a son, a daughter on the other end, with a story of debts, deaths and depression, and they could file it away as a suicide. But there was nothing. A simple case of a missing person, but they had the physical body – it was the person itself that was missing.

As to cause of death, Gavin's own theory had been a mugging gone wrong, a light tap to the back of the head in just the wrong spot. There was nothing at the scene to suggest a second party was involved, but the altercation could have happened elsewhere. In his mind's eye, he saw the man staggering across the sand, his vision darkening, sitting down to catch his breath. Then the results came through and said – what, that the man hadn't drowned, that there were no injuries, no evidence of foul play at all? Just a cancer so deep and vast that every step would be agony. Off the record, the pathologist's best guess was a heart attack brought on by stress and frailty, but she wasn't convinced by that theory either, and he could see how much the uncertainty annoyed her.

They had to tell the media that they had an unidentified body with an unidentified cause of death. Sometimes that can be useful – a detail in an article can jog a memory and bring a witness forward, or a family member might recognise a photo. They even reproduced the tattoos on the man's arms and chest, although they were mostly faded beyond recognition, distorted by a wasting illness into smudges of colour and black lines. All they got was their own words reflected back at them, a fuzz of white noise. It was as if a whirlwind had swept the man across the world and spat him out on this tiny beach in the middle of nowhere.

Some distance inland, there is a whale skeleton in the corner of a field. The largest vertebra is dented in the middle like a cushion and framed by the white arch of two rising ribs; the old folk claim it is a wishing chair. As the story goes, the animal was thrown into the sky in a storm, to fall with a thump so loud that floors shook throughout the village. In truth, Gavin suspects the bones were heaved there by pranksters. But as he gets older, certainty drains out of him like a slow puncture, and a flying whale is the least of what he could believe. He once read that all manner of things – blackbirds, fish, snakes, even sheets of clotted blood – can rain from the sky, spiralling downwards to catch in tree branches or splash against concrete. Scientists blame waterspouts, algae, colliding flocks of birds; they scoff at witnesses who stare at them with dull, exhausted eyes, who know that there is more strangeness in this vast, vast world than can be explained away.

And after the rain, Gavin presumes, someone like him is sent to clean up.

Around October they got a tip, a young man who had seen one of the posters. They brought him in, and when he broke down almost immediately, they were sure they had a guilty conscience on their hands. But then he claimed not to have spoken to the stranger at all, just watched him walking along the beach. In the end, they had no reason to keep him, or see him as anything but a nervous, but innocent, witness.

His account at least tied in with what they had already guessed: the man arrived that day on one of the buses that stop on the cliff. The driver remembered picking him up in Belfast and dropping him off on the day in question, an incredible feat of recall after almost two months. His description led them to the ferries that come in from England, and they followed the CCTV trail backwards from the bus station to the port. The images are grainy, and somehow the man has managed to avoid looking at the camera at every point he was captured. Getting off the ferry, his head is down and he darts out of the queue to the left, towards the city, instead of going inside the port building. Probably because he didn't have a ticket in his own name – they tracked down all the manifests from that day and there was nobody unaccounted for.

The driver remembered the man having a backpack. He had even rung back months after his first interview to ask if he had said that the bag was purple. He had, of course, but memory can be funny that way. There was no backpack with the body; he must have got rid of it somewhere along the way, but by the time they had that detail, all the bins had long been emptied. It wasn't until months later that somebody spotted a local drifter with a similar bag. The guards took him in for questioning, but he was useless; he tried to pull a knife on them, and they had to stick him in a cell to cool off. If they had the bag itself, they could at least trace it by its logo or material, but that was another dead end.

The man paid exactly the right amount for the bus journey, which might suggest he knew where he was going, that the village was his destination all along. Or that he just picked a point on the map and paid with whatever change he had in his pocket. The very last images captured of the man are on the supermarket's CCTV. He posts some letters into the postbox in the wall outside the building, but then moves out of frame and disappears. Whether a confession, a farewell or an electricity bill, the contents of his letters have never come to light.

Mystery piling on top of mystery, clue against counter-clue. A thread of coincidences, or just each fact happening in a certain way, one after the other, and when you look at them expecting to see a pattern, you force them into unnatural, unreal shapes. At the inquest, the pathologist said the cancer in the man's brain would have affected his thinking, so all these 'clues' could just be the product of a diseased mind. His brain might have been breaking down, memory and language fragmenting into a thousand pieces. Maybe he thought the KGB was after him, or a herd of pink elephants. Maybe they were.

Then, the dead man's wife appeared with a photo of the two of them together, and it had seemed like a glorious flash of light. She recognised the facial mock-up that they had sent out through Interpol, and Gavin had been ready to worship at the altar of forensics once again. But it had all fallen apart. The French police were so far up their own holes, delighted to be solving a mystery that had eluded the Paddies, that they had skipped doing any background work. Flying the fraudster over as if it was a done deal, expecting a bouquet of flowers and medals all around. What a monumental blunder on Gavin's part, though, to let her go off with a bit of evidence; it had taken them ages to track her down again and get it off her. He was lucky to avoid an official reprimand. His supervising officer had accepted that empathy towards the 'widow' had led him to it, rather than incompetence.

She wasn't the only one to send them racing down the wrong rabbit hole. The internet sleuths are convinced of a global conspiracy, pointing to similar cases that have happened in other places, bodies that have appeared as if out of thin air. For months, the tipline has been buzzing with cranks convinced they have cracked the case. Their theories range from the stupid to the extremely fucking stupid, identifying the man as everyone from their missing dentist to an alien abductee to the Pope himself. One suggested the man was a concentration-camp guard, which just showed how shaky his grasp of time was. All the Nazi guards are in their nineties or long dead, Gavin told him, but still he wouldn't be convinced: all these elites are drinking kids' blood to live longer, who's to say they didn't get that idea from the Germans? *Immortal Nazi vampires, is that it?* Gavin roared at him, before slamming the receiver down.

Just in case, he has followed a few of the theories up, if only to keep on the good side of the superintendent after the disaster with the wife. But he has only found dead end after dead end, frustration after frustration.

So, nearly a full year after the stranger appeared on the beach, he has decided to stop looking. If something new comes to light, he will return to it, but for now he is closing the book. His district covers a large swathe of rural countryside; mostly farmland dotted with the occasional clumping of houses. There are other crimes and other places that need his attention; this village is just one among ten like it, each with its own miniature dramas. He has done his due diligence, that and more.

And, besides that, he cannot shake a lingering guilt. The man's behaviour – the clothes with the labels cut off, the dumped belongings, the lack of any kind of paper trail – suggests that he went to great lengths to cover his tracks, to disappear entirely. Who are they to argue with such certainty? When he thought they had finally found his wife, her grief had been a validation – they were 'closing the coffin in her heart', as the madwoman said herself. But now there is nothing left. No justification to keep picking at the wound. He is thirty years in the force, facing into retirement, and he has learned to let things go. Not every question gets an answer. *Sometimes that slate just stays dirty.*

Let dead men rest.

———

Then one bright morning, a man walks into the station, bold as you please, and says he has something to confess. That makes them sit up straight. Gavin nearly leaps over the table to take his statement, sure that this is the break they have been waiting for. He knows the lad, vaguely – or knew his uncle at least, and the nephew took over the garage a few years back. He is in his early thirties now, so not really a lad, but being a guard is like being a priest – even if a member of your flock is twenty years your senior, to you they're still a little lamb.

But once they get him into the interview room, it turns out that it isn't anything to do with the stranger at all, but rather the remains of the wreck that lies just off the beach. Gavin had been up to his eyes in that old case too. On the morning the ship crashed, nearly thirty years ago, he had been pulled out of bed by the coastguard. In the blinking dawn mist it was a black apparition against the familiar horizon, as hard and unexpected as a fist in the ribs. He was freshly qualified and hadn't known what to do, standing there on the cliffside, but his presence made other people think someone was in charge. That's a large part of his job, if he is honest with himself: providing the illusion of control in a world that runs on pure chaos.

Afterwards, the guards were dragged into the bickering between the shipping company and the harbourmaster, accusations about fault flying both ways. They'd taken turns filing reports through solicitors, which were just *he-said she-saids* dressed up in fancy language, another kind of domestic dispute. It went on for more than a decade. Then, at the height of the recession, somebody burned the damn thing down. He was almost relieved, even if the harbour-master was screaming blue murder, accusing them of setting the fire intentionally. That stopped all the litigations: the shipping company settled the civil suits against them just to get the hell out of there. The crew got a payout, and the galley cook even bought the café up on the cliff, which annoyed him, because he used to like getting a free scone there in the mornings. He is probably the only one left in the village who knows where she came from, and because of that she looks at him like a piece of shit on her shoe.

Sitting in the interview room, the man speaks slowly and clearly, as if this is a script he has rehearsed every day in the long years since. He claims to have started the fire, that he had lit a few sticks of wood and the flames got out of control. Worse, he thinks there might have been someone in the wreck with him, someone who didn't get out before the engine went up. He can't say if it was a man or a woman, young or old, whether he had spoken to this person or just glimpsed them in passing. Under questioning, he admits that he hadn't really seen anything clearly, just had the feeling that he wasn't alone.

Gavin leans back in his chair to stare at him, trying to think back to that day. When the flames died down, he had gone out with a crew from the fire station at the next low tide, went over the site with a fine-tooth comb. He knows for damn sure there wasn't a single trace of a body there. They'd even sent a scuba diver out to film every corner of the place. They played some of the footage in the hearings: a slow, claustrophobic drift through the dark water. But in any case, that was that – no body, no case, no foul.

When they tell him that, the man looks like a broken puppet. The energy that had pulled him into the station leaves him all in one go, and he slumps right off the chair on to the ground. They consider arresting him for arson, but what would be the point? A possible crime fifteen years old, committed by a teenager, on a derelict ship that nobody cared about? Every day, there's less and less of the old wreck left, and in another few years it will be gone altogether. Good riddance. Dragging that old business to the surface again would do nobody any good.

In the interview room, Gavin tells him as much. *Go home, lad.* The man opens his mouth to argue, but Gavin shakes his head. *Let it go. Let it all go.* He walks out the door, unsteady as a drunk, and Gavin folds up his interview notes, tears them in half, then into quarters.

Strangely, one of the sleuths trying to solve the mystery of the stranger on the beach has also mentioned the ship. A priest over in Australia, another crank seeing connections where none exist, even if he is better spoken than the rest of them. His message suggests that they look into a ship, the very same ship that is now chunks of iron rusting just off the beach. Gavin chased it briefly, but the ship's paper trail is convoluted; it changes hands and names often, and the fateful fire destroyed many of its records. There was some suggestion that it had belonged to the Russians during the Cold War, and it was then that he threw up his hands: immortal Soviet vampires were a bridge too far.

Why had the man confessed to the arson now? He had been a teenager, a stupid one, but a teenager all the same. Had he been waiting for a knock on the door all these years? And why hadn't he left town, rather than staying to look out over the evidence every day? But guilt can be strange that way. Gavin has seen men wake up one morning after a lifetime pressing down on the memory of abuse – of a priest's cold hands, of a child's broken body – then throw themselves into rivers. Others will beat their wife to death and claim innocence, even with the blood seeping between their knuckles. Guilt takes everyone differently, but it can stick around for years, festering, like a tiny fragment of dirt in a wound.

Lately, he has felt a heaviness in the air. In the barracks, the night presses in like a wet cloth over his face, finding the contours of his eyes and mouth. When he started out, the beat was stopping into ten different pubs along his route to make sure the taps were unclogged. Now there's a beating or a kill-ing or a sex crime nearly every month. And it's not out-of-towners − perfectly ordinary people who have lived side by side for a lifetime just suddenly up and attack each other, like wild dogs. Maybe these things were happening all along, though, and the guards just hear about it these days. That's a horrible thought: behind closed doors, people have always been as awful as they are now. The oceans are rising every year, everyone says, and it will only be a matter of time before this entire island is covered by the sea. Sometimes he feels like going out to the cliffs and jumping up and down a few times, encouraging a piece to break off early, like a tea-soaked biscuit.

Gavin has never married, never fathered a child. At first it was disinterest, then disbelief; the willing attachment of a tether to a kestrel, then complaining when it tears out your eyes. When he retires next year, he will receive a certificate and a cake, and then will face down a parade of empty days surrounded by empty people.

The new priest in the village, the one that took over when the dour old fucker died, is fond of an old Irish saying: *ar scáth a chéile a mhaireann na daoine*. People live in each other's shadow; we must shelter each other rather than live alone and suffer in pride. He seems a different breed from the fire-and-brimstone vultures of Gavin's own childhood, the ones that crippled whole generations and spat on the wounds, but well-meaning all the same. He wonders if the polite Australian priest is of that same breed, or the type that will lash you to a pole with ropes of sin.

He's not a big believer in any type of god – how could he be with the things he's seen? – but when all the world is wildfires and floods and disease, when the very planet is bucking them off like a badly broken stallion, it does seem like the end of days has begun. Perhaps the stranger on the beach was just the first of another plague: bodies will begin to splash down on the village like fat, thick raindrops.

And there will be nobody left to clear up.

the priest

On ships, men are who they are without women.

Or so he tells his small flock at the Seafarers' Mission, although he supposes the same could be said about the priesthood. Father Larry O'Toole has never had much to do with women, in any case. There was a mother, back in Massachusetts, and a sister: the first chilly and distant, the second hysterical and exhausting. Even in school he was known as the brother of the girl who was always crying about something. An all-boys' boarding school put paid to that; he could read for hours in the library and he only had to hear about his sister's dramatics at the weekend. His mother had seemed quite relieved when he announced he was to go into the seminary. She was too tired to deal with any more things falling apart – and God was eternal at least, unlike his sister's boyfriends.

It wasn't unusual, in their small Boston Irish neighbourhood, for a son to go off to the Church, although it was normally the spare and not the heir. But seeing as his sister seemed to have that all sorted out – five children with three fathers, as best as he can remember – his mother had ushered him off without an argument. He took to the seminary well, which was unsurprising. He had an excellent memory, consumed books like a starving man and was solitary by nature. He used to quip that his best friends were a thousand years old – saints and scholars both, channelling the Emerald Isle of his grandmother's stories. More, he had an almost uncanny ability to switch off and blend into the background, to sit and be still, which made a contemplative life come naturally.

Some years in an inner-city Boston parish only made him gladder of the sanctuary of the sacristy. Then, after the sudden death of his mother, and some financial bickering with his sister, a change and some distance between them felt right, if not necessary. Larry applied on a whim to the Seafarers' Mission, without knowing where on God's great Earth he might be placed. He imagined some great floating church that sailed around the world, giving the sacraments to pirates and marooned men on desert islands, like *Robinson Crusoe*. To his surprise, he was offered a chaplaincy, and he had to confess that he got seasick on canal barges.

The Monsignor had laughed at him when he explained this and described his vision of a floating church. *If only, Larry*, he said. *No, the needs of sailors are a little bit more mundane. How are you with batteries?*

Larry hesitated, feeling like he was missing out on some great joke. In his last parish, the teenage boys had made a game out of distressing him, confessing more and more lurid sins while struggling to keep a straight face. But what could he tell their teachers? Break the Seal of Confession to announce: these boys are making up wicked, wicked sins? And how exactly would you know how wicked they are, Father? No, it was better to keep his mouth shut.

It always does to have a great stock of batteries. The Monsignor leaned back in his chair to explain. These men have been at sea for weeks and maybe months on end. They get into a new harbour and have a few hours off. Not enough to go anywhere, or do anything really, so they have to stay close to the docks. All they want is a face to talk to that isn't part of their crew. A place to sleep for half a day and maybe have a beer and a chat. A floor that doesn't move.

And the ministry? Their immortal souls? said Larry.

Yes, yes, that too. But mainly batteries, the Monsignor added. *Better than gold.*

Port Bunbury in Western Australia is a small but busy harbour. Ships come and go, and colourful shipping containers swing in and out like the lower cars of some monstrous Ferris wheel. Workers fill it up and leave again. It is never silent, which suits Larry. Too much silence can be bad for a man. *The sea is silence*, a Malaysian worker told him in his very first month there, tapping his head. *Except it is in here.* Now, Larry makes sure there is always a jazz CD in the player, a choir singing hymns or even a soothing loop of bird-song. Anything is better than silence.

The Mission is a grey, concrete bungalow that houses dorm rooms, a large common area, a small kitchen and a chapel. The things it offers to seafarers are practical as well as pastoral. Food, drink, books and magazines. Extra clothes, internet access, local SIM cards for their battered phones, for the lucky ones who have a loved one to call. And batteries, of every size and shape, for everything from DVD players to remote controls to torches, just as the Monsignor had said. Although these days universal chargers are more useful, but Larry still keeps a box of batteries under his desk, because you never know.

The Mission even sells miniature models of the Sydney Opera House, despite it being nearly 5,000 kilometres away. The workers will get no closer to the city than the port bunkhouses, but their families don't need to know that. The men don't have the time or money to go further inland; more than a full day's shore leave is a rare and wondrous thing. The shop sells stuffed kangaroo souvenirs too, and koala-bear fridge magnets – although the only animals Larry sees around the docks are rats. The suggested price is paid, more often than not. The Mission is run off donations, and for all their reputation, sailors give freely. For every man who ghosts away after racking up a hefty phone and board bill, there is another who leaves his fortune to the Mission in his will, in gratitude for some small moment of solace, sometimes half a lifetime ago, half a world away.

As chaplain, Father O'Toole tries to create as many of those moments of solace as he can. He has counselled men driven mad by homesickness, those who have lost limbs and sometimes their minds, entire crews abandoned by feckless owners. He sat with a man at a computer as he watched a video stream of his mother's funeral, the connection fuzzy and weak. He has translated frantic messages to immigration officials, passed word to port authorities about faulty equipment on board or weeks of unpaid wages. He must be circumspect, though – he treats the titbits of information he is given almost as solemnly as if they were in the confession box itself. He asks questions, nudges, makes suggestions. That is all. Any more than that, and the priests of the Mission would be blacklisted in ports around the world. Even now, some ships will not let them board. The trouble the chaplains cause by seeing their crews as human beings – as more than walking, talking bags of meat – meat that costs and makes money – is not worth the hassle to the shipping companies.

So the men come to the white bungalow of the Mission instead, alone and in pairs – and they are mostly men, for which he is grateful, although he is seeing more and more women these days. Women at sea are unlucky, he has heard, but then again so is a priest – another reason why he lets the men come to him instead of trying to board. It's not that he has anything against women! In his last parish, there had been a number of female ministers who were very helpful with the cleaning and keeping the choir rotas in order. And, of course, there's Our Lady, who stands proudly in the window of the Mission, her face and white veil yellowed from the harsh Australian sun. Larry just can never predict what women will do or say next, and that makes him uneasy.

Ships are always female. These modern days, there is a move away from that, to be more politically correct. The booklets the shipping companies leave in the Mission now refer to ships as *it*. It is beyond the chaplain to look at a rusting 400-metre-long container carrier with 20,000 steel boxes on board and call it a woman. But if he says *it*, the seamen correct him, with the usual nonsense about a ship being a protective mother, or a guiding goddess, or a volatile mistress. Superstitious malarkey, he thinks. And anyway, shouldn't it be a man? Men are easier to predict. They eat, they sleep, they fight, they grieve. And sailors are men, but condensed. Wasn't it Cicero himself who said it? *There are three types of people: the living, the dead and those who are at sea.* Some of the people who come through the Mission's doors are closer to death than anything else. He has listened to a hundred stories of cruel captains, back-breaking work, cramped living conditions, malnutrition, even enslavement. Stowaways, sometimes; left at the next port if they're lucky. In colder waters, they are heaved overboard and their bodies are never found.

Each one of these monstrous container ships spews out pollution and waste, and they criss-cross the globe like knitting patterns, day in, day out. He finds it hard to scold the men for not using the recycling bin at the Mission, but there it is – if Our Lord could manage forty days in the desert, then he can keep rolling the boulder up that proverbial hill. And sometimes when a fully loaded ship gets to port after months at sea, the containers sell for less than what it cost to bring them halfway around the world. So the journey – the fuel, the effluence, the workers' months away from home – has been for nothing, for less than nothing. But that is how the world works these days, and these are the invisible men who haul the global economy on their backs.

He tells them that, sometimes, because he thinks it sounds grand: *you are hauling the global economy on your backs.* Once, he held a makeshift Christmas party for the dozen or so men who happened to be in port on the blessed day. One of the Filipinos taught him to say Merry Christmas in Tagalog, *Maligayang Pasko!*

After a glass or two of brandy, he tried to tell the men about his musings on the global economy, but the brandy had numbed his lips and he ended up having to mime the concept out. They went away thinking that the priest had given them each a magic backpack.

But why not? Sailors have always believed in magic. Changing the name of a ship is awful luck. Losing a hat overboard makes for a long, wet journey. Tattoos, too: a pig on one foot and a chicken on the other to help you float; a compass rose in black ink will lead you home. Five thousand miles for a swallow, ten thousand for two; polliwogs have to be rattled when they cross the equator for the first time. His own red, Irish-American hair is bad luck on board a ship, although they seem to let him off with that one once he takes out the box of batteries. No saying goodbye before a journey; that is one he has to work hard at. It is difficult to see the back of these men – who have cried, sang, slept under his roof, who he has sat with and helped gather up the pieces of a life – and watch them leave his flock without a word of farewell.

But these are the rules they must all follow, rules to keep the spell of safety intact. And when you get down to it, religion is just another form of magic. Different holy words, but at their heart, they all mean the same thing.

Dear Father, let me return home safe.

If I cannot, let me be remembered.

All anyone really wants is to be remembered.

Larry is not sure why he remembers *this* man, over all the others. Despite his excellent recall for hymns and scripture, he is not good with faces. And most of the workers have something liminal and interchangeable about them: a sense of transparency, like a thin and flavourless gruel. But from this man, he had the odd feeling of a fast-moving object that had suddenly come to a shuddering stop, the ripples still expanding outwards, the stalled object vibrating with displaced energy.

The man is sitting at a computer in the alcove opposite the small chapel. The chapel is technically a sacred space, marked out with a square of carpet and chairs rather than incense and pews. The altar is very rarely used for services, and the chairs are regularly reassigned to the long dining table in the centre of the room. Larry has never said a full Mass in his years as chaplain in Port Bunbury. Most of the visitors think that even being in the presence of a priest is enough, as if salvation is something you pick up through osmosis.

The three computers, by contrast, are so well used that the keys are worn down from the pressure of fingers. Larry feels he can sometimes track what the men are doing by the movement of their hands and the expression on their faces, despite the fact that they are often typing in a language he has no knowledge of. And some of the things they look up … not that he would begrudge a man his corporeal needs, but there were places in town that would look after that side of things! Some of them are worse than the teenage boys in Boston – he has to put on headphones to block it out. But mostly, he leaves them be and sits behind his own desk, gets on with the business of tending to his small yet ever-changing flock. His ability to blend into the background comes in handy here, where the soft noises and rustling of his work become part of the tapestry of noise in a port.

The man at the computer is so still that Larry hardly notices him. The steady click roll, click roll of the mouse is interspersed with the whining of the out-of-date processor. From his desk, Larry can only see the profile of the man's face. He is probably in his late sixties, older than most of the other workers – although it is a job that quickly turns young men into old – with uneven grey hair and a crooked nose. He looks pale, with sagging eyes, as if he has been below deck, away from the sun, for a long time.

The man feels the eyes on him and looks over to the desk. Larry lifts his hand to wave at him, *let me know if you need anything*. He turns back to his notes; he has been asked to write down a few words for a newsletter that goes around to all the Missions. The previous edition had a feature on ship-breaking, the remote places where ships go to die. It is a horrible business full of toxic chemicals, horrific injuries, disposable lives; even children that work under cover of darkness. Often, the workers go into small spaces – cargo holds, duct keels, chain lockers – without enough ventilation. The rust on the metal causes a chemical reaction that sucks all the oxygen out of the air, and they suffocate. Or drown. Drown without an inch of water.

The article was informative enough, he supposes, if a little unnecessarily morbid; he has resolved to send in something lighter for the next edition. But now, he is trying to think of an optimistic anecdote, and nothing but a grey stretch of time comes to mind.

The CD in the player comes to an end and there is a stretching of silence before the next one settles into place. The click roll, click roll of the mouse becomes loud, louder. The printer struggles to life, belching and whirring, committing black words to paper one line at a time. Larry writes a few lines about a man who brought along a harmonica for an evening and sang a Bob Dylan song, despite otherwise not having a word of English; about how music is the universal communicator. Yes, that sounds most excellent. He circles the words *universal communicator* as a possible topic for his article.

Father.

He is startled up and away from his desk by the sudden voice; his pen spins out off the edge of the table and across the floor. The older man retrieves it for him, bending slowly and painfully, as if each movement is tender and disconnected from the last. Larry can see that he is missing one of his fingers; a common injury, or so he has heard, in an industry where ten-tonne masses of steel constantly grind against each other, often taking whole limbs if not entire lives. Up close, his face is narrow and the sickly paleness of his skin draws circles under his eyes. The smell of the man is familiar, but it takes him a moment to place it. Larry has done his fair share of wakes and funerals, even without an embalmer's perfumes ghosting around the room, but he has never before smelled this from a living, upright person. It is the hot, tired smell of a fever overrun: a game that has been lost.

Father, the man says again, his voice hoarse and raw, his English accented but fluid. *A blessing?*

Larry shakes his head instinctively, then quickly changes it to a nod. *Of course, my child. Is there anything in particular you have on your mind?*

The man smiles and slowly opens his arms, managing to encompass in the gesture the vastness of the world; the winding, pitted road between birth and death; the weight of simply living in this Vale of Tears.

Forgiveness.

Father O'Toole stands up and walks over to the little chapel. Dips his fingers in the font of holy water and makes a rough sign of the cross. The man sits creakily on a chair in front of him, bows his head. Larry mutters a few generic blessings: a plea for absolution, a lifting of spiritual weights, the hope for a better tomorrow. The man nods his head, his fingers gripping the sides of the chair. Larry rests his hand on his shoulder before leaving him with his thoughts. He takes a walk around the docks in the freshening breeze.

Once, on a brief holiday to Jakarta, he visited a market and saw a beggar sitting at a small metal table covered with a thin layer of sand. The man seemed almost disinterested, and Larry couldn't understand why the cap at his feet was filled with coins. Then a speaker below the table began to throb, a deep and steady bass beat, and the metal began to vibrate. At first it was chaos, a twitching mass of ants, but then, oh! the mandala began to emerge, stars and diamonds and squares, concentric circles that met and cross-hatched and faded.

He worries sometimes that long ago the Creator, like the disinterested beggar, sat back to watch the patterns in the sand. But these thoughts are kept down below, in the shifting acid of his stomach, where they settle and dissolve. Every so often they rise up again, in bile and in blood. He tastes them now.

He suddenly wants to spread the word, to assure this poor dying man that no judgement is coming down from above.

But when he comes back from his walk, the man is gone.

———

The next day, he is back and asks Larry to order him a taxi to Perth airport, two hours north. He is unsteady on his feet, like a frond of seaweed in a turning tide, and in the daylight the marks of a hard life are even more visible. He is clutching some pieces of paper; Larry recognises the scritches of yellow ink that mark everything that comes out of the Mission's misaligned printer.

Can I drive you to the hospital instead? Larry asks suddenly, surprising himself. He takes care never to offer too much, to wait until the men come to him with their needs. But what this man clearly needs is medical attention, a hand to hold, not the trauma of a long flight to who-knows-where. The sick man shakes his head, thanks Larry for his help and goes to wait for the taxi outside. He only has a single piece of baggage, a deep purple backpack, with his shipping company's branding across it in large white letters. It is one of the older companies, but still, Larry knows their colours and logo by sight, and their poor reputation. Even in an industry where people are treated as things, there are some who manage to treat them as less than that.

He sometimes wonders what the value ratio of human lives to shipping containers is: how much tiny, incremental amounts of increased suffering is caused by the cheapness of the global trade; how many lives are actively made worse by the sale of some product or another for a dollar less. If only there were a magic backpack after all, he would give it to every man who crosses the Mission's threshold. Maybe *magic backpack* would make a good title for his next article … he makes a note of it.

He considers checking in with a contact of his at the shipping company, making sure they are aware that a member of their crew is leaving, but he already knows it is just a passing thought that he will not act on. *Primum non nocere*, and all that: this man may be eloping from an overly punitive contract, an unpaid wage or maybe debts in the other direction. If anyone official asks, he will tell them the truth, but he will wait to be asked.

Besides, the man seemed so certain, so fixated, as if each movement he made had been long-considered and refined to use only the minimum amount of energy from a finite source. Larry feels a strange kind of envy at that certainty in the face of death, and, for the first time in years, he resolves to phone his sister, to look up his diaries, to remind himself of the names of his nieces and nephews.

As the taxi pulls up, he finds himself drawn to prayer. Yesterday's musings are gone, swallowed deeply again, and he addresses the Almighty with the same prayer he says at funerals:

Into thy hands, oh Lord,
we commend the soul of thy servant departed.
May this sailor find repose
with the sea in which he gave his life
that we might live.

After the car drives away, he checks the log on the main computer to see what was printed out the previous day. This nosiness is unlike him – he has been burned before, found horrid, explicit images that gave him nightmares – but curiosity has him by the lapels now.

He recognises the printout from the feature on ship-breaking in last month's newsletter; a short few paragraphs on ghost ships that were probably intended as a light-hearted aside. It describes a frigate that accidentally ran aground on a sandbank somewhere off the coast of Ireland, caught fire and has almost completely disintegrated. The image accompanying the article is blotchy and pixelated: the outline of a beached ship, and in the distance behind it, a small, cliffside village that curves around the sea.

the fallen

It is 1985 and the English have come to steal their fish again.

Their trawlers prowl the North Sea, filling their nets, then scuttle back home like cowards. Gunnar's father sits in his chair, drinking *brennivín* and roaring about the thieving English. The old man is too brittle to go to sea again, and lame besides, but he is proud of his son for fighting for Iceland. This time, though, it is not a war of bullets and blood, rather of spaces and words, treaties and broken promises. Politicians shake their fists over invisible lines on a map and argue about fishing zones. His father fought this same war in his time, as a fisherman, trying to tear entire shoals out of the sea before the foreigners came to steal them. But Gunnar is an engineer; he has seen what decades hauling lines have done to his father's hands, so he chose the machines instead.

Engine rooms are dark, and hot, and so loud he wears two sets of earplugs. When he is at home between contracts, his wife tells him not to shout, that she can hear him just fine. But he loves the noise that turns liquid and runs into your bones. Only when the noises change is there a problem. A new hum, an elevated pitch, a barely audible clunk – those are the things he dreads hearing. The radio buzzing, a call from the bridge – *why can you not keep the engine tame?* He wants to scream back at them, sometimes, over the crackling radio line. They expect an answer, a reason, but an engine is a thing alive. So too is a ship, but an engine is the beating heart of the animal, with chambers and tubes that are constantly trying to block and twist themselves into knots. And an engine is always trying to die. His job is to prolong it, to drag out the life through oil and chemicals and even words – yes, words; he talks to it, coaxes it, urges it on. Nobody can hear through the din in the engine room.

And even if they did, all sailors are a little mad.

––––––

One night, Gunnar comes up for some air and finds a man on the foredeck, alone. The ship is driving hard into the flat water, the bow kicking off dual waves of white foam, like a dog with a bone in its teeth. The air is as cold and sharp as brittle bones, and the plumes of the man's cigarette smoke rise directly up as if drawn to the heavens by a magnet. He is younger than Gunnar, dark-haired with rough features, and wears a thick ring on one hand; Gunnar's father would roar to see such foolishness. He doesn't know the other man's name and doesn't ask. As a rule, foreigners do not interest him. The coastguard has had to enlist ships and men from abroad to face the mighty behemoth that is the Royal Navy. Even the ship is foreign, a frigate hired from the Russians; the signs in the engine room feature harsh, angular letters that mean nothing to Gunnar. He knows his work well enough to not need the signs, but it still unsettles him, as if the ship is screaming something in a language he cannot understand. The crew is mostly made up of mercenaries – Germans and Argentinians and Russians and Swedes – privately hired and privately paid. Their task is to escort the coastguard, bulk out their puny fleet on their patrols around the fishing grounds. They are not officially there, and their engagements do not officially happen, but men with money will always find ways to protect it.

Gunnar is the only local aboard, hired to give their rough mission a veil of legitimacy. He is quiet by nature, and rarely talks to the other men. They speak to each other in English; Gunnar speaks a little, enough to get by. They joke about Icelanders, about their glumness and deadpan gazes. But it is not that Gunnar doesn't find things funny; it's just that the other men expect him to arrange his face in a way that is unfamiliar to him. Besides, he is an engineer, not deck crew, so he spends little time upstairs with these men. Navigation is not his business and he is glad of it. At night, everything is translated into lights, big and small, blinking or constant, moving towards you or floating away. You must track each of these lights, and the darkness where they are not, while underwater currents and cross-hatching waves fight you every second of every day.

But on this night, the sea is flat, the air calm, and it is almost quiet, except for the squalling of a flock of Arctic terns. Gunnar stands beside the man and wishes him a good evening in English. The younger man grunts, doesn't turn to look at him, but offers a cigarette. They watch the gentle licking of the waves against the hull. Gunnar leans on the railing and asks the question that has been on his mind since he saw the amber glint of the wedding ring as they ate silently in the mess: who is the lucky woman so ferocious she would spot his infidelity halfway across the globe?

The man laughs proudly and says it's not for her, but for him; a reminder of what he has to go back to.

Gunnar snorts at the recklessness of youth. He is thirty years married and does not wear a ring; his wife does, he thinks, at least when he is home. What she does when he is away is hers alone. *That ring will take your finger off one day*, he says.

The younger man shrugs, raises his palms outwards, as if to say: what will happen will happen. *One day* is as far away as the edge of the world. *Look* – he says suddenly, pointing to an area of sky – *Cassiopeia rises*.

Gunnar has never had the patience for sky-watching, even when the aurora danced above his village as a child. The skies at sea are the clearest in the world, but on the rare occasions he is out on deck at night, he keeps his head down. The stars are too close and too far away: join-the-dot constellations, dirty smears of galaxies, nebulas that faintly remember colour. His father once told him that the sky is a sea of infinite stars, a solid wall of light, but most are too dim for their light to reach Earth. If he looks up for long, he gets the sense of falling from a terrible height, but also rising, rising like a submerged cork, and if he keeps staring up, he will burst through the surface of the sky.

He squints where the hand is pointing. *Where?*

A woman, on a chair. The younger man's fingers trace the ghost of a jagged shape. *And from there, the Pole Star* – his hand rises to a bright point of light then drops down – *and the Great Bear.*

I do not see a woman, Gunnar insists, annoyed now. *Or a bear.*

Here, the man says, rolling his sleeve up. Around his elbow, there is the same jagged outline, with a long tail that leads up towards a single point on his shoulder, then dips to a ladle of stars. The tattoo is new, the lines sharp and pitch-black but still healing around the edges.

Gunnar looks from the ink to the stars again, tries to match the shape around the bony protrusion of the man's elbow to the sky. He nods, although he still cannot see it. He lights another cigarette and looks firmly out to sea. Surprisingly, the other man doesn't speak again, doesn't try to prolong the conversation or force it into an uncomfortable shape. Usually, younger men talk and talk and talk. It takes a lifetime to understand the value of silence.

———

Their time in the North Sea is mostly quiet, with brief excitements – if an English trawler crosses too far into their waters, a coastguard ship passes astern with a trawl wire-cutter, snipping the net and entire catch loose. Besides that, the most they do is threaten to barge each other, and the English usually back down in the face of the Icelanders' hulls, which are reinforced for ice-breaking. The job of their frigate is to loom above the foreign fishing trawlers, to blot out the skyline with missile docks and aged anti-submarine sonars left over from the heights of the Cold War. Once, they fired a round across a trawler's bow; Gunnar felt the throb and shake of it from the engine room.

The days stretch on, and fewer and fewer British ships appear on the horizon. Those that do have fled by the time they make it over, leaving a seething patch of sea. There is politicking going on, back on shore, between the two governments. Gunnar does not understand it and does not care to. He stays below and works the engine. That is his job. Its two diesel shafts and gas turbines are noisy – Soviet-made and unreliable – but the ship herself is fast and sleek; she can move through calm water as silently as a gull.

He meets the other man frequently, at night, although he is young enough to be his son. Gunnar and his wife have no children, and he has never felt the lack. They do not talk much, preferring to stand in silence, smoke and look at the stars. Any wisdom Gunnar has gained is in his hands, not his words. He believes it is easiest between men when there is a problem to be worked on, a too-tight valve or a door to be unstuck. But slowly, they begin to pull sentences out of each other. Eventually, Gunnar tells him about his uneasiness with the night sky, the awful sucking emptiness of it. The man teaches Gunnar to find the shapes between the stars, to trace animals and buildings and people out of them, and slowly, gently, the fear lessens. Gunnar tells stories about his wife, his village, about the white-smoked cod that his father and father's father grew up on.

The cod are dying, now. When he was a child, they would have leapt out of the water. But the Americans and Canadians and English have ruined it all; fishing and fishing with their monstrous nets that dredge up the entire ocean and destroy all the small lives of the sea. Now, even on board, they must eat frozen lumps of whiting instead of fresh cod, and patrol for foreign ships. Gunnar wonders how the ship feels about her demotion, from Cold War to Cod War, from nuclear annihilation to the small matter of fish.

The anchor line is clanging. Bang rattle bang, all night long, right behind his cabin. The vibrations get into Gunnar's head and shake his thoughts loose; his dreams have been so violent and vivid of late that he wakes dazed, sure he has committed some awful act. It takes until he splashes his face in the sink before the curtain of dreams is washed away.

The anchor isn't used often; there is no need at sea and at port they come alongside and tie off. On the rare occasions they are ahead of schedule, they still don't anchor – instead steaming slowly into the wind, then drifting back, then steaming again, for however much time needs to be eaten up. But for some reason, the metal line has been left unsecured. Gunnar's cabin shares a bulkhead with the chain locker, and the thud, slide and clank keep him awake. The noise doesn't happen every swell – there is enough of an unpredictability about it that he can't get used to it. It is not easy to get used to noises at sea, but it is a necessity. The buck and roll, the whir and putter of the engine, the slam of hatches and doors as watches change every four hours. Some alert system in the body gives up, decides it can't keep up with the hundreds of sights and sounds and feelings that on land would be an imminent threat. Young seamen live on their nerves. Old seamen have very few left, and Gunnar can feel himself becoming old.

The rattle and clank of the anchor wakes him yet again one night, and he sticks his head out of his cabin and staggers into the mess, where the other man is writing letters. He looks up sharply as Gunnar fumbles with the heavy metal door, then down again when he realises who it is. He doesn't ask why he is awake when it isn't his watch. Gunnar doesn't ask him why he is awake either.

He wedges himself into the corner of the sofa and tries to sleep. The lull and the rock of the waves. When he wakes up, he is alone.

———————————

In the morning Gunnar asks the man to help with the anchor chain.

He says no at first; they must wait until they dock in Reykjavik, two weeks away. It is against procedure to go into the anchor locker while at sea, despite the fact that there has not been a sighting of a British ship for many days.

Another two days of sleeplessness and Gunnar comes to him again; his eyes weeping with tiredness and frustration. The younger man sighs and agrees. There is no need to tell the captain or to mark it in the log. It is a small and neat job that will be quickly done: they will wrap a rope around the anchor chain, tether it to the hull. It will be silent, and Gunnar will be able to sleep.

They move up together through the ship, red-eyed with tiredness and annoyed at each other for the misfortune of existing. Through the hatch to the fore-castle, and over to the loose boards covering the small opening to the anchor locker. The chain pools here, rises through the windlass, then out to the lashing and down through a pipe to the anchor itself. The opening into the locker is only hip-width apart, and there is a ladder leading down into blackness.

Gunnar stares into the dark of it and is taken back in time, sees again his family's smokehouse. The squat building sat at the bottom of the laneway, and every year they smoked armloads of fish to last them through the winter. He would help his mother rub the curing salt into the deboned fish, the white flakes burning the rough patches around his fingernails.

Then his father would hang the cod from hooks inside the smokehouse. The doorway was small, so as not to let the heat out and the snow-laced wind in. When the hatch opened, the smells of sea, tar and woodsmoke twisted together into a fug so thick he felt his fingers left tracks in it. But the awful opening itself, the dark hatch, was a shaft that dropped away to the centre of the earth, and Gunnar was terrified.

He cried the first time he saw his father disappear into the entrance to tend the wood that needed to burn steadily for days at a time. When his father came out, he cried harder; tears of relief that got him a cuff around the ears. But the next day, when they came to the smokehouse to check on the fires, his father knelt in front of him.

Listen for my song, he said. And sure enough, once the hell-hatch closed behind him, out of the dark, squat building would come a wordless song. Gunnar would wait in the cold, but he would not cry, and his father would come back to him by the end of the song.

You or me? the other man asks, raising a coin. Gunnar shakes away the memory. The coin is unfamiliar, the letters as alien as those in the engine room. He taps one side and sighs when it reappears on the back of the man's hand.

You.

Gunnar snatches the spool of coarse, blue rope from the man's shoulder. He bends down, sticks his head through the hole until the blackness inside turns to stained-glass red, the light refracting through the ship's crimson hull. He can see the unsecured anchor chain coughing and twisting like a dying fish. The opening is tight, but he slides in with some effort; his feet find the rungs of the ladder and his fingers curl around the lip of the hatch. He wraps the blue rope around his waist to flatten his boilersuit to his body. The other man looks down on him, nervously checks his watch.

Past the rim of the hole, salt-corroded metal falls away under Gunnar's fingers. The red begins to tint everything, like his eyes have been dipped in rust. He looks up at the bright-white opening, just a metre above him, and realises that something is wrong. His lungs are not working properly; they are tight and whistling. He opens his mouth to call out, tries to lift his arm above his head – it is heavy, so heavy – his friend above him is crouched down, with his shoulder and arm shoved through the hole to reach Gunnar, his sleeve has bunched up and around his elbow. Somebody is screaming for help but it is not him; the air comes out of his mouth in a creak, like a log of wood splitting under an axe. His brain is drowning, shutting down, refusing to do what it is told; his body is a thick, dumb animal, falling into darkness. He does not feel the impact of the floor.

Gunnar reaches up a final time, up to his friend's stretching hand, up for the stars around his elbow.

But the red is rising fast and he is moving in slow motion; the noise is draining away and he worries for his engine, just once, and then the line of red, like water trapped between two panes of glass, has filled up and is tipping over.

The last thing he sees are the two sets of eyes above him: the blinking hatch hole and his friend's, white and bulging in fear and panic, eyes within eyes within eyes.

Don't be afraid, he tries to tell them, *I'll sing.*

the daughter

She first speaks to him one night in Murphy's bar. It is July, that liminal time between the end of exams and the announcement of the results, when the future is balanced on the edge of a piece of paper.

Nessa has only just turned eighteen, although she has been going to bars for years; she has always looked older than her age. The walls are covered with ugly posters and not a single piece of furniture matches another. She prefers the clubs in the city, but the barman here is known to be loose-eyed when it comes to IDs, even more so since he got engaged to his boyfriend a few weeks ago.

He is sitting with a crowd and there is a tiredness radiating out from him, as if he is a dully throbbing lightbulb on its last legs. He is thin, with a jumper that doesn't suit him, and thick, wild hair. She recognises him from the supermarket, where she and her friends would gather at lunchtimes, eating chips from the café next door. She had watched him work with a vague curiosity, but she could see his disinterested gaze glance off her like a flat pebble off a pond.

Nessa is surprised to see him in the pub; each time she has seen him outside of work, he has been alone. She knows some of the boys with his group and can tell that he is new to them too; they clap his back and try to include him in their stupid, childish jokes. She can tell that this closeness of people is already chafing. She has always had a knack for this, for seeing the frailties that others try to disguise; it makes her desperately sad, and then angry, in a way she can't quite understand.

As people rearrange themselves around trips to the toilet, she ends up sitting beside him. She introduces herself and asks his name, pretending not to know the answer.

Mitchell. He formally shakes her hand, as if they were meeting for the first time at a funeral.

Nessa. He smiles when he repeats her name, but it is only half of a smile; the other half is somewhere else, along with his attention.

Someone arrives with a platter full of tequila shots, which wobble dangerously and then spill into a sticky waterfall that lands on the front of Nessa's dress. The others all roar dramatically at the loss, *taxi, taxi!* Then the spiller leans forward to grab the sodden fabric, announcing he will drink the booze anyway. Mitchell shoves him back with the flat of his palm as Nessa shrinks away in disgust.

They share a cigarette, afterwards. It is windy and wet, so they have to pass the lighter over and back. Nessa waits. If he asks if he can buy her a drink, or calls her beautiful, she will hate him. There is something about compliments that sets her teeth on edge, makes her want to prove the person wrong by squelching her face into a horrible shape or tearing her hair out. But they smoke in silence, sheltering from the rain.

As she stubs out her cigarette, she thanks him. He looks surprised.

———

She was six years old when her neighbour called her over to a hole in the fence, pulled her close and whispered: *your mum chops up dead people.*

She ran inside, begging her mother to deny it, to say that all she did was put plasters on fingers and fix sick tummies. Instead, she sat Nessa down and explained that she was like a detective; it was her job to figure out how people died, so their families could know what happened to their loved ones. Sometimes that involved looking inside their bodies, taking out the parts and seeing what exactly went wrong. Nessa, in the bright, sterile light of the kitchen, felt her fear fade away and curiosity take its place. *Do you put the bits back in? In the right order?* Her mother had laughed and assured her that she did. But for the rest of the day, all Nessa could think of were the puzzle-pieces of her body, and what would happen if one were to be left behind.

She cried the first time she got her hair cut at a salon and the dead ends were swept into a bin. The hairdresser laughed and called her a sweet little thing, gave her a red lollipop. That night, she had a nightmare about the ends being mixed up with others – grey hairs, black hairs, coarse hairs, curly hairs – a swirling cauldron of strands dyed a hundred shades. She reached in to retrieve her own but slipped into the running stream and was dissolved. Ever since that, she has always brought a tuft of hair home with her, gathering it up furtively from the folds in the smock that the hairdresser drapes around her. She always loses it afterwards, of course – she is as proud as a cat and as untidy as a dog, her mum says – but it is the taking that breaks the spell.

When she was thirteen, her dad found her in the laundry cupboard in the middle of the night, clutching her knees and rocking over and back, feverishly counting the towels. It felt like her eyelids were made of lead, and every time she moved her pupils it took an age to drag them from one side of her face to the other. She was terrified that she would be stuck in slow motion forever, living in quicksand while the world around her went on at a normal speed. Her mother tried to shake her awake, but she was already the most awake she had ever been, and she was terrified.

A hazy few days in the hospital and an emergency appendectomy later, she was home, still slightly woozy. When she gingerly sat down on the couch, her mother had produced a white-capped medical container and handed it to her, smiling. Nessa hadn't asked for it, hadn't even known it was possible, but her mother knew the paediatric surgeon from medical school, and had begged a favour. Her appendix floated in a clear liquid bunched up in parts and gristly, like something left over after a Sunday roast. She turned it around and around, holding it up to the light as her dad made her a cup of tea and a hot-water bottle.

Then, when she was fifteen, she let a boy come inside her for the first time, and she felt like she was stealing a piece of him away forever. The other girls at school didn't understand the power of it; they called her a slut, wrote her name on the back of toilet stalls. She couldn't explain it either. If she could find the right words to shape around the feeling, they would call her worse things, so she added to the graffiti instead: giant tick marks and love hearts and smiley faces. Sometimes she wrote foul things about herself, words so sharp and ugly that the other girls reported them, and the cleaner had to shuffle up the stairs to bleach them off. Once, in the mirror of a shop window, Nessa saw the sheen of desperation in her own eyes, like there was a trapped animal inside her. That night, she had pulled off her fake nails one by one, bruising the beds and tearing the cuticles.

Soon after that, her mother announced they were moving away from the city and out west, where life would be slower and more concentrated. Her parents expected her to feel some way about this move, about losing her school and friends and community, but it had felt trivial to her, like changing an outfit before a night out.

Now she is eighteen, in her final months of secondary school, and the world sits on her shoulders like the too-small shell of a hermit crab. Next year, she will go to college, or maybe abroad; she hasn't decided yet. She might be a lawyer or a hairdresser or an engineer or a pole dancer. She could be the best in her year, if she wanted to be, which pisses her mother off. She could do anything she wants. But most of the time, she doesn't want anything at all.

Sometimes she dreams that yellow-white pus seeps in from the ocean, a rising tide of it, as if the polar ice-caps had melted all in one go, but instead of water there is a thick, milky fluid running down the street, rising above doorsteps and windows until they are left stranded, on the top floor of the school – and their teacher insists on them going over quadratic equations, or formulas, and all the while, outside the window, the off-white tide is rising.

―――――

One day in June, just before their final exams begin, the rain is lashing the school windows like the tail of an angry cat.

At lunchbreak, the other girls make a performance of popping open the buttons on their skirts and stretching their bellies, arguing over who is the fattest, the ugliest, the hairiest, the most disgusting. They circle around the same topics again and again, never asking new questions, never expecting new answers. Today it is the fact that a stranger died on the beach last summer and has still not been identified. For some reason this excites people; they are desperate to make it seem like a mystery rather than a meaningless death on a meaningless day in a meaningless place. The girls move on to ways to die: poison, immolation, asphyxiation. They agree drowning is the worst way to go. It makes Nessa angry to hear these silly girls talk about it, as if they know anything, as if they *understand*.

She asks her mother about the case one Friday night, after her father has gone to bed. Three-quarters of a bottle of wine has disappeared over the course of the evening between them. Sometimes they talk like equals on these evenings, when it is just the two of them, rather than fighting like opposing ends of a magnet. Her mother is all facts and logic; Nessa feels things so deeply and heavily she expects their weight to tear through the lining of her stomach.

There are things her mother won't talk about, like when she has to go to court, or appear in the news, or when her phone rings in the middle of the night. She keeps the practical workings of death wrapped up in her files, out of reach and under control. So it is a surprise when her mother doesn't ignore the question.

Instead, she sighs. *I don't think we'll ever know what happened. And I have to accept that.* She smiles, a little tipsily. To Nessa's discomfort, her mother reaches over with one arm and hugs her, tightly, as if they were two drunks in a nightclub bathroom. Then she gets up and goes to bed.

There is one glass's worth of wine remaining in the bottle, but it is left untouched on the coffee table until morning, and the base leaves a red half-circle against the fine oak grain.

———

She sees him again on the cliffside overlooking the beach a week after they meet in the bar. Nessa has come into the village to get something for her mother.

A scab has formed between them – it is fresh and thin and will break if the skin around it is stretched, but it is there.

She recently found her appendix in a jar on her desk after causing a minor landslide in her layers of memories. A pile had grown around it – scarves, photo frames, bracelets, empty make-up bottles, birthday cards, ticket stubs – things that burned with significance when she first put them there but turned dull and silvery-grey over time. The lump of meat in the jar looked disgusting: white and diseased, with pieces floating around it in a hazy cloud. She fingered the small scar on her abdomen, tested it for weakness, but the red line of old pain seemed stronger than the untouched skin.

In biology, she learned that each day, thirty trillion cells in her body divide and die; she becomes a new person, inside and out. It is a revelation to her, this shedding and renewal, like peeling off a sunburn and eating it, letting it stick to the ridged top of her mouth.

She threw the jar out.

She sees Mitchell sitting against a dune on the clifftop and stops, pretending to consider the new monument that is being built on the grass behind her. The artist is working on it in stages, but the rest of the time, it is cloaked in canvas. The wind lifts the fabric, showing a glint of bronze, but Nessa does not pay attention to it. She is running through a hundred scenarios in her head. She could casually walk past him, drop a coin or pretend not to recognise him. She could catch his eye and wave, then pretend she was waving at someone else. She could sit on the grass downhill from him and take off her jumper so he can't help but see the shape of her.

Then some burst of purpose sends her forward and suddenly she is sitting down beside him. Below, the marram grass sways, the beach is a glistening crescent moon, and the oyster traps stand in a proud line. In the distance, seals are sunning themselves on the sandbank beside the remains of the wreck. From here, the lumps of metal look like the clean, dark bones of a beached whale.

Behind them, the canvas covering the monument whips in a wind that suddenly shoves at their backs, towards the water. A flock of sanderlings flashes over the dunes like a hail of bullets, ducks low to graze the sand, then disappears out to sea.

It takes a second for him to notice her, to return from wherever he was – somewhere out on the cliff edge, or further, over the horizon. And then, like a spinnaker whipping wildly before it catches the full strength of the gust, his mouth twitches, expanding outwards into a full, true smile.

the dead

The plaque is covered with names, but there are hundreds more of us than could ever fit on a square of metal. Thickly etched lines of words and dates list those who went into water and didn't come out. At the bottom, there is an empty space left for new names. This morbid conversation echoed around the council's design meeting: how much space should we leave, how many more will we lose? What amount of grief and loss and wailing can we fit on this plaque? This is forward thinking, as well as back, to plan for inevitable breakages in the stock of lives by the sea.

Above the plaque is the freshly completed monument: a bronze ship's capstan with six bars radiating out from a central column; a tool to multiply the hauling of many hands. Instead of a halyard, the spokes of the capstan are draped with fishing line made out of metal, hard to the touch instead of billowing in the wind. Caught in the nets are small tokens of flotsam and jetsam: a pipe, a crate, a log of driftwood, a child's shoe. A bronze lifebuoy sits at the foot of it, and a flag runs up a steel line, its halyard whipping at the sky. Gaudy spotlights peeking from the grass will keep the wet shine of metal alive, even in the darkest night.

The sculptor is a stranger to this place, born and bred in cities, but he visited once or twice to get a sense of the air, and thought it enough. The pieces were made inland but brought here to be assembled into a whole; it took six arms and a winch to lift it into place. The artist spent weeks in the fenced-off area of yellow plastic at the top of the cliff, heating the metal to seal it together, watched by children who asked questions and then grew bored. Lastly, the sculpture finished, the council provided this plaque, to anchor it to the cliffs, and then he drove away, back to the clatter and noise of the city.

The last name on our list is fresh, the laser-etched lines a lighter silver compared to the weathered brass of the old. It is not a name, rather a description: *unknown*, and the date of his passing, a full year ago today.

Above the names, the dedication reads:

FOR THOSE FALLEN AT SEA
AND THOSE STILL FALLING

And today, on this dappled August morning, there is a time of remembering. A crowd gathers around us, in fits and starts, on bicycles and on foot, in vans and cars. A few trickle up from the church down the hill, followed by a priest in black flapping robes and white-bright runners peeking out from under the fringe. The crowd comes from north, south and east, always moving west, towards the monument that looks out over the ocean. It is a speedy gathering; all in attendance are local and know by heart the time it takes to reach the green on the cliff. Too early and there will be an awkward wait before the ceremony, a dilution of the moment; too late and it will all be over. They line up in a horseshoe, stepping backwards to make space for latecomers, so the circle expands and widens with every new body.

Somebody lays out a wreath of candles in a bed of red paper flowers, but the cliff-wind is taking the flames as soon as they light. Men do not shake each other's hands, but toss their heads back in greeting: *how's the form? Ah, sure not dead yet.* Women shove hands into their pockets. The sky is bright and wide, but a memory of storm rolls through the few leftover clouds.

Children weave in and out of the crowd, grasping at trouser legs and skirts for balance, and slingshot off again into the game. Older children pick their way down on to rocks; they make crab lines the old way, with a lick of mermaid's tress-weed for string, a holed stone for a weight and a whelk beaten off the wall for bait. One finds a treasure: a cuttlefish shell. She is frightened, a little, because the shell suggests something ancient, something prehistoric. She snaps the cuttlebone in half to find layers and layers of white, calcified waves, the entire ocean condensed, the memory of floating, not falling.

Time ticks on and the crowd shuffles uneasily, unsure of what to look at. The message that went out across the wires was simple – there will be a minute's silence at noon on Sunday to celebrate the opening of the monument, in memory of those who have been lost at sea. Watches and phones are checked and checked again – they are not synchronised, and time flaps free and untethered. Nobody claims ownership of the message that beeped in their pockets just a few hours earlier. Nobody steps up to take charge, to say we are *here* and the time is *now*.

Finally, the sound of the slow church bell rings out across the town: an electric tolling, programmed in; there are no hands left to pull the ropes. There is a chuckle at this divine pronouncement of time. The noise of the crowd shudders away unevenly as the minute's silence begins. A dog barks and is shushed. A baby whines, then laughs. There is a clasping of hands, and an unclasping; fingers stuffed awkwardly into pockets. Heads bow, some in prayer, some in memory. The priest looks up at the sky, but it is so bright he must close his eyes.

You remember us.

———

Some of us were lost on a fishing trip during a spring tide. The first oar we cried and flailed for; the second we had no energy to mourn. We sang as we waited for morning, a bawdy song about breasts and holes. But come dawn, it was silent; there was no land, no birds. We could see the dark arch of the lighthouse, but it was a world away, and there were no slick, grey dolphins to shepherd us to shore.

Some of us were lost when our great, hulking galleons foundered on hidden rocks. Those foreign sailors lie with us too, their beards tangled with seaweed. They saw only wild men when their Armada first landed here, but across the centuries we have come to a knowing of each other.

Some of us leapt overboard, iron shackles around our ankles, rather than become slaves to heartless men. Others were kept chained belowdecks at the docks before sailing into the horizon, without even a glimpse of this green shore. We watch the others who come now, hidden away in too-small boats, seeking refuge. They pay dearly for hope, but bodies are money and money is bodies; this has always been the way of it.

Some of us boarded coffin ships and were overcome by the sight of familiar mountains fading away. It was not the leaving that broke us, but what we were leaving behind. Hunger and shallow graves, hunger that melded our bellies with our backbones. Others made it further, across the wide Atlantic, and died there: a vicious bout of typhoid, the fists of a drunken master, hanged guilty for a murder.

Some of us were buried by our crew with a shovel and a loaf of bread, in case we weren't quite dead. But the tide was turning, and the captain would not wait to be sure. We woke, under the soil, but our bodies rolled over and returned to slumber, as if life itself was the bad dream.

Some of us were the watchers on shore; we leapt at the sound of a bleep into orange drysuits and sped around the bay, pulling summer-swimmers from the water and towing stricken engines home. We died on land, but our ashes went golden into the sea as heroes.

There are children here too; they came floating out on puffed blocks of plastic, sunburnt and dry-mouthed. Others have been here a thousand years and have not grown a day. Our years are both endless and flash by; we are freed from the deep channel of time.

Some of us left our own children behind. Wives. Husbands. Teenage sweethearts. Fathers, mothers. Sons and daughters who broke our hearts again and again with wild ways, but could mend them with a secret smile. Friends and neighbours, houses and homes, sorrows and sicknesses; an ache in our chest that we needn't have worried about at all.

One of us died in a small anchor locker, reaching out for the hand of a friend. And now, that friend has come, a lifetime later, to make amends. A lifetime of running and working and suffering; a lifetime where memory stole joy from every careless moment. A wife abandoned on shore, children that were never born; a promise remembered with a simple band, even when it tore flesh from bone.

Guilt is a weight, a leaden chain; it can morph and stretch itself to fit every space, like the supple frame of a cuttlefish. But guilt has no heart and cannot live forever: each heartbeat destroys a little universe, brings another one into life.

Your doctor says that the final name etched on the plaque is not one of us, that he was not lost at sea. That his heart simply decided to lay down its weight. But we claim him as one of our own, because, no matter the cause – a sad, wet end, a violent cut, a quiet slipping away – all our hearts have laid down their weights.

Death has many pieces. At the very end, our lives fractured themselves, and the shards swam away to where they belonged. The still-living carry those parts around with them: kind words and gentle skin-touches and sweet, sweet tears. The best parts of us are elsewhere, spread out across the land in a fine mist of memory. Our voices are the last thrumming of an insect's wing on a web.

All that lodges here is the shape of our ending.

After the full minute has passed, the silence stretches overlong, as if the first to break it will draw down a curse on themselves. The wreath of red flowers flaps loudly, and the sound of waves crashing against rock becomes clear. The priest is the first to open his mouth, and he shatters the stillness ungently, bellowing out the words in a deep baritone that belies his small stature.

I thought I heard the old man say,
Leave her, Johnny, leave her…

The crowd is startled by this sudden stamping of noise on the carpet of silence. A child laughs at her own fright and raises her hands out towards the sound of the song. Some stretch their heads high to see who is singing, and their shoulders hunch uncomfortably at the sight of the priest in his flapping black robes; an old-fashioned envoy of the yoke of his god. But this is not a song of god, of worship, of punishment. It is a song of people – a song to ease the haul of a rope, the turn of the capstan, the chafe of an oar – a song for the here and now, for those who are still alive.

Tomorrow you will get your pay,
and it's time for us to leave her.

The priest finishes the first verse before anyone joins in. His voice is slightly out of tune and his face is scrunched up as if he is staring into the sun. But his enthusiasm fills up the crowd, and other voices join – men, women, young, old – and a wave of song rushes over the land as you find the familiar words of the chorus.

Leave her, Johnny, leave her,
oh, leave her, Johnny, leave her.
For the voyage is long and the winds don't blow
and it's time for us to leave her.

After the song ends, there is an attempt at reviving it for one more verse, but a kind of communal chuckle filters through the watchers, an unleashing of tension, an embarrassed laughter. The melding together of memory begins to dissipate; the crowd is unmoored and let drift away. Hands drape around shoulders, conversation ripples out from small groupings, plans are made; the week ahead is fresh and full of possibility.

A sudden gust crackles against the halyard unsecured on the flagpole, a familiar rattle-rattle that once meant fear; signalled a stormy voyage that, for love of money, could not be postponed. A fleet of by-the-wind-sailor jellyfish litter the shore, their delicate structures like blue-tinged fingerprints. Among them, a seal is beaching itself in exhaustion; a man with a van will come again first thing tomorrow to take the fallen animal away. More will join us at our post, but for now, for the everlasting now, there is life.

See! The wind is filling up the sky, the clouds are lifting, and the sun falls golden on the sand, the remains of the wrecked ship, the seals hauled out to doze, the lighthouse, a beacon of tomorrow and yesterday. The red dot of a fishing boat moored to see out an earlier squall. A changing of seasons. A changing of times.

See! The ocean is lifting higher too, tufts of salt and white horses leaping from the crest of waves, trying to reach the sun. The wind runs across lips, the chafe causing dry skin to crack and the taste of salted blood on the tongue. The wind curls around the cliffs, lifting scarves and hair and flapping cloth against limbs, bringing tears to eyes. Some in the crowd cry out or point at the sudden gust – look! The dune-grass ripples and bellows; a great whooshing roar that dives from the rocks and into the vast, vast ocean, slipping out towards the horizon.

Here is where the world ends.
Have you ever felt so alive?
Have you ever felt so alive.

226

Author's Note

Huge thanks to the Arts Council, who awarded me a Literature Bursary in 2020 to begin this book. In 2022, they granted me a Next Generation Artist Award, which will allow me to begin a new one. After I get some sleep.

This book involved a lot of research, most of which I did not use, despite my best efforts. Some of my sources include: Rosita Boland and *The Irish Times Atlantic* podcast for excellent journalistic work; Marie Cassidy's autobiography *Beyond the Tape* for insights into the role of a pathologist; *Down to the Sea in Ships* by Horatio Clare and *Deep Sea and Foreign Going* by Rose George for their accounts of the shipping industry; *Cod* by Mark Kurlansky for learning about the Icelandic Cod Wars. I am also grateful to Sligo Harbourmaster John Carton – my mishearing of 'Cod War' as 'Cold War' set some cogs in motion. Also the annual Wild Atlantic Shanty Festival, which closes with the song mentioned in the final chapter.

Mostly, I took facts and twisted them to my liking. They may groan under the strain, so any errors – practical, logical or creative – are my own.

My home county of Sligo provided much of the inspiration for the landscape in this book, especially the wild places. The setting itself is fictional – an amalgamation of countless seaside villages around Ireland – and the inhabitants are all my own invention. A ship *was* set on fire in Sligo harbour, but that story is far more interesting than the one I have told here.

This novel features characters from different cultures all over the world. Although I have tried to imagine their lives with nuance and respect, I will have made mistakes, and I plead ignorance rather than malice.

The deaths of the two men at the beginning and end of this book are inspired by tragic, real-life incidents, but their backstory is purely fictional. Despite what you have read here, and in full recognition of the hypocrisy, I believe the dead should be allowed to rest.

———

My personal thanks go to many people.

I am hugely grateful to my father, who helped me access many useful documents, and has an unwarranted amount of faith in me. My mother, for her kindness, and her insistence on wrapping everyone she meets in it. My three sisters and brother, four nieces and nephew, for a providing welcome distractions. My extended family – the power of the Armstrongs and Mayes united could move mountains.

Friends, writers and otherwise, for their help with the plot and early brainstorming; CoFo, for their usual genius in deciphering my nonsense; Misfits, for literary troubleshooting; IWC Evolution, for solidarity.

Friends in Sligo, Dublin, the UK, America, Australia and elsewhere. I am my own worst enemy, but you helped me call an occasional truce.

My agent, Marianne Gunn O'Connor, for her patience – early drafts of this contained every idea under the sun, and she gently helped me pare it back. Dan Bolger, for helping me find a throughline to hold the story together.

All at Bloomsbury – editorial, design, production, marketing and sales – for guiding me through my second book and producing such a gorgeous finished product.

This book was written during the most difficult period of my life, through lockdowns, heartbreak, sadness and sickness. I hope some of those ghosts can now be laid to rest.

229

A Note on the Author

SHEILA ARMSTRONG is a writer from the north-west of Ireland. She spent ten years in publishing and now works as a freelance editor. Her first collection of short stories, *How To Gut A Fish*, which was longlisted for the Edge Hill Prize, was published in 2022. *Falling Animals* is her debut novel.

A Note on the Type

The text of this book is set in Bembo, which was first used in 1495 by the Venetian printer Aldus Manutius for Cardinal Bembo's *De Aetna*. The original types were cut for Manutius by Francesco Griffo. Bembo was one of the types used by Claude Garamond (1480–1561) as a model for his Romain de l'Université, and so it was a forerunner of what became the standard European type for the following two centuries. Its modern form follows the original types and was designed for Monotype in 1929.